All royalties from the sale of this book will be donated to Africare.org, a charitable organization that works with local populations to improve the quality of life for people in Africa.

To the young women who are the hope
for peace in South Sudan

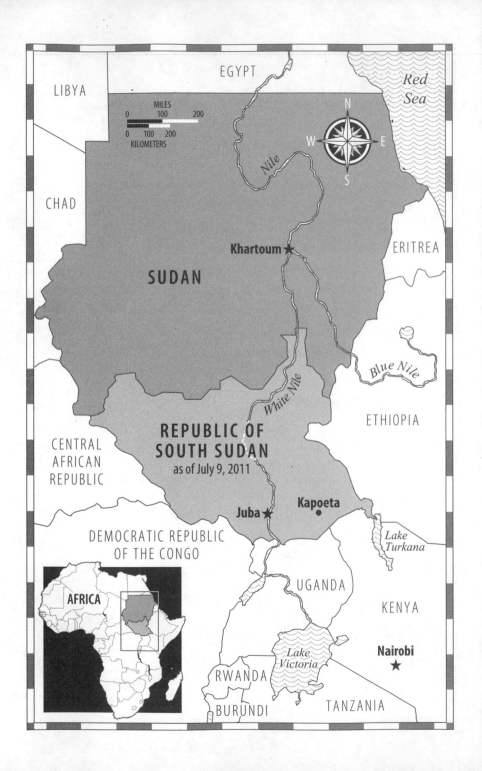

LIBYA

EGYPT

Red
Sea

MILES
0   100   200

0   100   200
KILOMETERS

N
W   E
S

Nile

CHAD

Khartoum ★

ERITREA

SUDAN

Blue Nile

White Nile

ETHIOPIA

REPUBLIC OF
SOUTH SUDAN
as of July 9, 2011

CENTRAL
AFRICAN
REPUBLIC

Kapoeta ●

Juba ★

DEMOCRATIC REPUBLIC
OF THE CONGO

Lake
Turkana

AFRICA

UGANDA

KENYA

Lake
Victoria

Nairobi
★

RWANDA

BURUNDI

TANZANIA

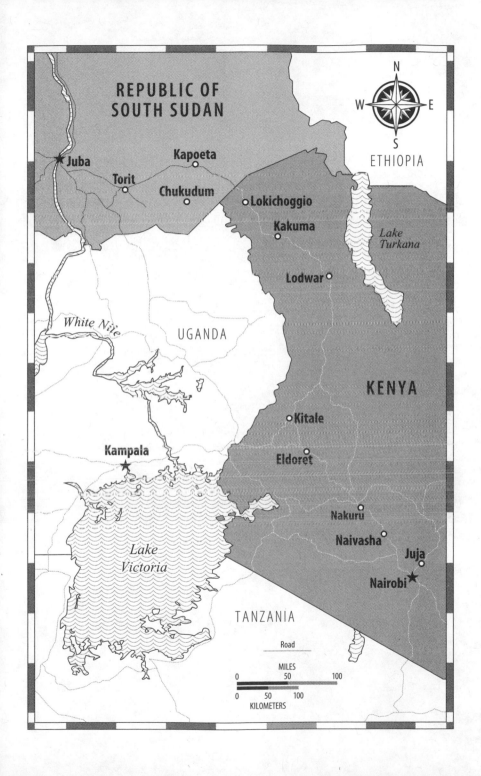

—1—

THAT ONE THERE? We call her Nadai. Nadai's voice is as pure as a batis bird's when she sings. Though she is three years older than me, she lets me climb up with her in the mango tree.

"Nadai," I cry. "Let down your very long arms and pull me up." And she does have the longest arms — thin but strong as rope.

"See how I can make the mango tree laugh," Nadai says, and she shakes the branches, which makes several mangoes fall to the ground.

We eat the mangoes then — juice dripping down our chins — juice that Nadai wipes off with the inside of her wrist rather than her fingers. Nadai's tongue is long, just like her arms. It makes me laugh.

It is Nadai who tells me things, Nadai who first shows me where the mouth of the mango is. Some mangoes have skin that grows yellow or pink on the outside, but here in Chukudum we grow Indian mangoes. Their skin remains green even when ripe. It is only by prying open the mouth of the mango that you can see inside.

"Poni, you are a hungry, hungry girl," Nadai teases.

It is true. I can eat mangoes down to their last meaty string.

"Did you eat breakfast, Zenitra Lujana Paul Poni?"

Nadai's legs dangle from the tree branch. She flaps her arms up and down as though she is a heron preparing to take flight.

"Mama fried a goat liver for me, and I ate it right up then ran all the way to school."

"You run everywhere."

This is the joke, my running. The women in my village entertain themselves by constantly sending me on errands. "Run and fetch some water," they tell me, and then they laugh to see me sprint off like my heels are on fire.

"Why walk when you can run?" I say.

We stay up in the tree for hours. Below us, we hear the *clackity-clack* of children dropping round stones into holes in rows as they play mancala.

Another group of boys play football using a dried lemon for a ball. If they are lucky, one of the women will needlepoint a ball out of an old sock, since the lemons often split apart. When the boys score a goal, we throw the dark leaves of the mango tree up in the air to celebrate.

I like watching these boys. In particular, I like the way the goalkeeper stands, swaying back and forth, his eyes watchful.

So that you should know the truth about me, I am not only known as a runner but also as a troublemaker. Perhaps this is why I like Nadai. Like me, she is always eager to go to the forbidden river. "Kinyeti River, Kinyeti River." We say it only in whispers.

Kinyeti River is where everything happens — where the

women go to bathe, wash clothes, scrub dishes and share news. Yet this river is greedy. It eats large numbers of children every year when its waters are high from the rainy season. Some adults call these children sacrifices.

And do not forget the crocodiles. These beasts mainly keep to themselves, but every once in a while, one will draw its wrinkly body out of the water — its eyes as still as stones — and, with a snap of its jaw, carry someone off.

Mama calls the river Disease Soup, since it is filled with nasty illnesses. My father has told us we may not go to Kinyeti, not ever.

Yet how can we stay away from a river that is so much fun?

Once there, my brothers, Iko and Lotiki, coax me knee-deep into the water.

"It's not so deep," they say. Then they push me in all the way.

I hear a swooshing noise as the water yanks me under. My ears pound, and my throat burns. I kick and thrash at the water, which is like a python squeezing the air out of me.

Finally, I fight my way out, coming to the water's surface with a pop. I continue to paddle my feet and arms crazily as my brothers cheer.

"Now you're swimming," they yell. It is as simple as that.

Later, they say they wouldn't have let me drown for too long, would have waded in and pulled me out eventually, but this is how children are taught to swim.

I hate the river yet want more of her.

I sneak away to the river whenever I can and, when I do, I decide that I want to be like those boys and girls who can swim with a mat made of reeds held high above their heads. If the mat hits the water, it falls apart, letting the others know you weren't strong enough to make it across. I try a few times, but every time I can make it only part way to the bank before my mat floats away in soggy pieces.

Nadai finds another way to prove her bravery, jumping into the water from the bridge that sits so high above it. For a brief moment she is dancing through the air, her body that of a dark fish that has been thrust out of the water. She screams as she makes a loud slap that cracks open the surface of the water and sends her plunging down.

We play, all of us, for hours, but because I have swallowed so much river water, when it is time to go home my brothers beat me around the stomach until I vomit. They do not want my father learning about Kinyeti.

My father is a clever man, though, a highly respected chief and pharmacist. When we get home, he takes one look at our red eyes and the white mucus that is gathering in their corners.

"Did you go into Kinyeti?" he asks.

"No," I lie. But then, as I am talking, I can't help myself. I give a shivery sigh. It creeps up inside of me — the result of all the cold water I gulped and vomited.

This one teensy little sigh is enough to tip my father off.

"You went in," he says, and this time it is no longer a question. Secretly, I am impressed with the way he is able to read me, the way he stares me down.

That night he canes me using a thick branch that he has carved smooth. *Whack, whack.* My whole body aches from the beating. It is awful, and it is worth it. I know that I will return to Kinyeti.

■■■

WE CHILDREN ARE constantly on the move, roaming among the tukuls, our round huts with cone-shaped roofs. Most of our free time we spend outside, climbing trees and exploring. It is not that there are no chores. All of my mothers have me wash the dishes so that I can practice bending my back. They have me carry small loads of twigs on my head so that my neck will grow strong, strong enough for the day when I will carry an entire jerry can of water on my head, or a full load of firewood.

When Lodai Giovanni arrives one dry afternoon, all of the women start dancing and jumping. He has come to claim another wife. Because he is wealthy, it is assumed that no one will reject his offer of cattle, goats and blankets.

When he announces that he has chosen Nadai's family, her many sisters start gossiping. They wonder which one of them will be married off. At this time, Nakidiche, Nadai's mother, is far away, gathering firewood. It is no matter, since marriage negotiations are done through the father and uncles. In fact, Nakidiche will not learn of her daughter's marriage until the arrangements have already been made.

I see Lodai Giovanni walking towards Nadai's hut. Giovanni is an Italian name, a gift from the Catholic missionaries, added to his Didinga one. Despite the lovely name, he is not pleasing to the eye, with a big bald spot and his hair parted on either side as though the Israelites have passed right through it. He is highly respected in the vil-. lage, but he is also a man in his forties, married with many children.

Lodai Giovanni points at Nadai.

She is only twelve, has just had her first month's bleeding. I hear the women whispering to one another, "Used to be, during the time of peace, that men waited until the girls were older."

Nadai does not look up. She continues playing by our favorite tree. It is only after her uncle puts his hands around her waist that she realizes what is happening. She wraps those long arms of hers around the tree trunk.

Nadai's uncle says a few words to her. At first he talks gently, explaining that this is her duty, that this is the way her mother was married. When that does not work, he simply rips her off the tree.

She screams, "No, no, no," as if she is being attacked by wild animals. "Father, how can this be?" I don't know whether she is calling to her own father or God himself, but her cries mingle with the ululation, the hoots of the women in the village.

We children look on, watchful as hunters.

As Nadai's uncle drags her past me, I notice the inside of her arms where the skin has been scraped off in her desperate attempt to hang onto the tree.

Suddenly, she catches my eye. I see her look. *Do something, Poni.*

But what can I do?

No time is wasted. The villagers slaughter a bull for the couple, rub perfumed oil onto Nadai's skin, then take her into Lodai Giovanni's hut. I picture Lodai Giovanni — his skin as old and tough as animal hide, his belly soft and low-hanging — and imagine Nadai having to lie down with him.

Women change once they get married. I have seen it happen. Overnight, Nadai is no longer a girl who can play in trees. She can no longer attend school. Instead, she remains with Lodai Giovanni's other wives, has to serve him dinner, has to kneel down. The other wives teach her to compete for Lodai Giovanni's attention. They teach her to obey. It is rumored that if a husband does not beat his wife, he does not love her. Some of the older wives say, "Is it true that your husband does not love you enough to pay you notice? To beat you?"

I rarely see Nadai after she is married. When I do, I poke out my tongue, hoping she will show me her long one. But she simply nods sadly and turns the other way.

I remember that look of accusation in her eyes when she was dragged away. *Do something.*

—2—

NADAI TRIES TO KILL herself three times. Twice she attempts to hang herself from a tree. The first time, the rope does not hold. The second time, she is discovered, taken down and beaten. The third time, she eats some purple poison berries, but all that does is make her ill.

I think she is too strong to die, that one.

Only eleven months after she is married, I hear screams like those of a wild dog coming from the birthing hut. One of the women tells me that it is Nadai giving birth. Women are not supposed to scream out during childbirth, but Nadai does not care.

But when I come back later, there is no noise coming from within. It is then that I see the midwife leaving. There is blood on her skirt.

She makes a circle with her thumb and first finger.

"The birth opening was too small," she says. "There was too much blood." She has such bony, narrow fingers. I can't help wondering if this comes from having to reach inside so many women to pull those babies out. She shakes her head sadly back and forth.

"Nadai?"

"She and the baby died. The baby will be called Ikidak."
Ikidak is the name for all dead female babies.

I can't believe it. Nadai, who climbed trees so easily,
whose body refused to die even when she tried to take her
own life, is dead? I imagine the baby, a wet lifeless pile lying next to her. I don't want to see this picture in my head.

Pretty soon, around the village, I hear women wailing
and sounding out the death cry.

For the Didinga, when we hear the news of a death in the
family, all the relatives go and smash everything in the hut
— break the pots, pour the grains and flour onto the floor.

I watch the way the undersides of Nadai's mother's arms
tremble as she picks up a pot and hurls it down. Next Nakidiche picks up handfuls of grain and throws them onto
the ground. The grain scatters and rolls like beads.

While no one is looking, I reach down and pick up a
small shard from the shattered pot and put it in my pocket.
Throughout the day I take this piece out and slowly drag it
along my arm, wanting the sharp pain on my skin.

When I see Nakidiche a week later, I call to her.

"What?" She looks up at me, her eyes as slow and unsee-
ing as a fish's. It's clear she does not know me at this moment. Then, after what seems like a long time, she finally
takes me in.

"Ah, Poni. You were a good friend to Nadai."

I want to say how much I miss her, how playing in the
mango tree is not the same now, but I remain silent.

"I have many daughters, you see, but Nadai was special." She pauses and wipes her eyes with the sleeve of her
dress. The sigh that comes from her is big enough to rattle
the ground. "Nadai was the one I sang a special morning

song to. She was the one I let lick porridge straight out of the pot." I picture Nadai, her long tongue, her look of mischief. "Now she is with God. The baby, too."

I cannot explain it, but I am disgusted with Nakidiche. I hate the way she stands there, her shoulders limp as a cloth doll's.

"Why didn't you save her? Why did you let her marry that man?" By all rights Nakidiche should beat me for speaking to an adult in this manner, but she looks too worn.

"How could I, a woman, stop the marriage?"

There was nothing Nakidiche could have done. She was not even there when it took place. Still, I am angry at her.

"You should have tried harder," I yell. In fact, it was me Nadai begged for help, me who watched her get dragged away. My insides ache, and my throat hurts. I have never yelled like this before, not at anyone, not even my brothers. Certainly my mother would never allow me to raise my voice to her.

Nakidiche pulls up her dress and grabs the soft pouch of her stomach. She shows this belly to me, shows me without using words that there was a time when Nadai inhabited this flesh of hers. Now all that remains of her daughter is this stretched-out skin — scars like claw marks across her belly.

I don't want to view her horrible stomach. Instead I turn and run away.

Usually we children look forward to funerals. My brothers have been known to ask hopefully, "Anyone go to God this month?" Funerals mean a big celebration with lots of songs and food, and sometimes a goat or even a bull slaughtered for the occasion. It is said that funerals bring together even the worst enemies. We celebrate the person's life as we mourn their death.

Nadai's death, like all children's deaths, is different, of course — completely lacking in joy.

Nadai should have fought harder. Had it been me, I would never have let go of the tree, no matter how hard my uncle pulled. I would have held on until my arms pulled off.

This is what I tell myself.

—3—

HOW MANY WIVES does my father have? Good question. My father has four official wives, yet we know he has more than this. My uncle says six, my mother says twelve. Naturally, he does not live with all of these wives. Some of them he just visits in neighboring villages.

Because we have a large family, there are always children at our compound. For a time I don't even know which ones I am related to by direct blood. But my own mother, Mama Nahoyen, remembers each ancestor in our complex family. She is the one who knows the who and what of our family, the one who makes certain that, when a marriage is going to take place, a man does not accidentally end up marrying his sister.

To map out our kinship ties, my mother draws a series of imaginary lines in front of her, lines like strands of spiderweb.

"You see, this one is the brother of that one, and this one is aunt to that one," she explains, stretching her fingers apart and holding them in front of her face. Our family is like a tough math problem, but Mama can figure out the answer by looking into her palms.

Despite the fact that I sneak off, I am supposed to be the trustworthy one of our family. I am only ten the first time Mama puts me in charge of the house while she goes into a neighboring village for a few days.

"You are the girl in charge now, so take care of your brothers."

So I do. While Mama is gone, I take over some of her chores. I turn pumpkin into stew, grind grains, fetch water and feed my brothers. I grow accustomed to Mama's comings and goings, but I still ache when she is gone.

When Mama returns from visiting relatives, buying soap and other goods, I cling to the backs of her legs as if in doing so I can pretend that I was there with her on her journey, magically hooked onto the backs of her sturdy calf muscles. I want to lick the mud right off these legs.

I am always with Mama when I can be, but sometimes I visit with my other mothers, too. Of all my mothers, Nakanoi is the toughest. She rarely has any food for us to eat and is only nice if my father is standing nearby. Natibol, another one of my mothers, is good to me. I like her large shoulder blades and the way her back is so straight when she carries firewood on her head. Also, she has a particular way of glancing over her shoulder at me when she dances that makes it seem like she is sharing a private joke.

Of all my mothers, though, my own mother is my favorite. This is not always the case with us. Some girls prefer other mothers to their own, but not me. Mama is the one who calls me by my special nickname, Chi Chi. She is the one who makes me laugh. She has a giggle that goes "Eee-heh-heh," and she tells the most entertaining stories about animals who make the same mistakes that humans do, who are too vain like the flamingo or too gossipy like the square-lipped rhino.

My father is usually away traveling, visiting his other wives or pharmacies. But when he has a guest to entertain, he always brings him to Mama. My father knows that Mama is the daughter of a chief and knows the proper way to treat esteemed visitors. She knows which language to use — Latuka if they are from Torit, Taposa if they are from Kapoeta, Bari if they are from Juba, or Arabic if they are from Khartoum.

I watch how Mama acts around guests. She casts her eyes down, kneels to serve food, then disappears out of sight and commands me to do the same. Around the men, Mama is like a shy deer, but when it is just us girls, she turns back into a lioness.

Like all Didinga mothers, Mama beats me from time to time. It happens like this.

First, Mama lets me know she is angry with me for something I've done by giving me a look and a click of the tongue.

"Take care," is all she says. "The next time it will be bad."

In her head, Mama apparently keeps a running tally of how many offenses I have committed. She doesn't share this with me until I have committed one too many.

At this time, Mama begins to list all my wrongdoings in order from first to last: "You see, in the past week you forgot your prayers, did not wipe your feet before entering the hut, then told two lies." I nod and try to look ashamed, thinking this is the end of my punishment.

But later, when I come inside, I see it. Mama's cane lying on the table. This means I am about to get a beating. Sure enough, Mama grabs one arm and slashes me with the other. I curl my toes as hard as I can to keep from crying. I don't look into Mama's eyes, not wanting to see the look of disappointment in them.

After she is done beating me, Mama gives me some tea with sugar. She does not hold a grudge. In her mind, the slate has been wiped clean, which means I can start in on new mischief.

Though I stay with her the most, Mama always tells me, "I'm your mother, but so are all these other women here." What she means is that anyone can beat me if I misbehave. When it comes to us children, we can't do anything bad without one of the adults noticing.

There are so many eyes watching me.

My cousin Keiji plays with me from time to time. She does not attend school like me. Instead, she spends much of her time fixing her hair or giggling over the local boys.

Though Mama does not approve of this behavior, rather than cane Keiji herself, she says, "I will leave it to God to punish this girl's foolishness."

When Keiji is no longer nearby, Mama tells me, "Some girls are like that, born silly."

"And me?" I ask. "How was I born?"

"Fierce," she replies.

Mama is always giving me advice.

"Treat the cows as well as you treat your family members."

"Yes, Mama."

"Stay away from puddles of water at night. This is where the mosquitoes gather. Daytime mosquitoes usually don't cause problems, but evening mosquitoes carry diseases."

"Yes, Mama."

Sometimes Mama's warnings are about health, but her other warning is more of a plea. "Do not become me," she tells me, her voice turning low and raspy. "I never attended school, and now you must feel sorry for me. I never got an education, but you must. Otherwise you, too, will end up on your knees."

■ ■ ■

I AM WALKING home one evening through the cool mist that always hovers around my village when I see one of my mother's best friends, Chocho, hiding in some bushes.

"Auntie? What are you doing there?"

When Chocho emerges, her face is covered with wet leaves. She looks like some type of bush creature. I almost laugh, until I see the blood seeping out from under the leaves. Chocho doesn't say a word, just turns away and walks towards her hut.

Later, I tell my mother what I saw.

"Her husband beats her, that is why," Mama replies.

"Then why did she return to him?"

Mama looks at me as though I should know better.

"Where else would she go? If she leaves him, her family would have to return the cattle he gave them for a bride price."

Without warning, Mama yanks my hair hard.

I cry out. "Why did you do that?"

"Let that be a warning. Stay in school. Never marry early or let your husband beat you."

I want to protest that I am nothing like Chocho. The boys should be frightened of me, not the other way around. Rubbing my sore scalp, I decide it is best not to argue. I may not be afraid of boys, but Mama is another story.

Later that night, my older brother Lotiki starts in on me, teasing me about my dirty feet with that gruff low voice of his.

"Poni, Poni, not even a bath will clean you. You are muddy through and through."

In response, I slap him hard across the face. His cheek reddens, while my hand tingles.

Abuba, my father's mother, is staying with us. She sees what I did and hisses out a single word, "Kali." Wicked. She then continues to give me an angry eye, even after I shrink away.

Abuba is right. I know I have a dangerous temper. Yet how can I explain to her how good that slap felt? How can I explain the thrill of it?

The next day I wake with sweat above my lip, my whole body hot as boiling soup.

Malaria. I know without being told. I try to curl my toes against the pain, which feels like bee stings up and down my body, but even this is too much effort. Instead I lie on my mat, letting Abuba's declaration about my being wicked echo through my head. I am the one who has made myself sick. My temper has ignited the flint within me, and now I am filling with fire.

I hear my mother talking to Abuba in her hush-hush voice. "The fever is too high. Pray." These are the last words I hear before I enter a dream in which burning grass scorches the backs of my legs.

Days pass, but I have no desire for food.

Mama makes a mixture of tree bark, groundnut shells and plant roots, a medicine my father taught her to make. Though he is a pharmacist, my father has always believed that traditional cures are best.

"Chew this," Mama commands, sticking the paste under my nose. But I do not have the energy to talk or to chew. Mama grabs my bottom jaw with both of her hands and forces my teeth to move up and down. Then she clamps my mouth shut until I have no choice but to swallow. The taste is so, so bitter, but I cannot even make a sour face.

I fade in and out of sleep, but I am never comfortable. I am too hot, too weak. I am beginning to fade away, I think to myself.

Mama prays over me. "God, help Poni. Pour strength back into her."

Even through my haze, I can feel the force with which Mama prays, the way her body shakes. She squeezes the sides of my head with both her hands. Perhaps she is trying to squeeze the illness right out of me.

All I want to do is escape the heat of my body, to sleep, and yet something keeps pulling me back, back to my mother and her hands.

Every time I strain my eyes open, there it is, Mama's face looming so large over my own.

In the end, Mama's prayers are stronger than even the most bitter medicine, and gradually they work their magic. The heat slowly seeps out of my body, leaving me limp but calm.

It is only once she sees that the malaria is gone that Mama stops squeezing and shaking. She continues to sit on the edge of my mat. But now, rather than praying over me, she tells me stories.

My favorite is the one about the two brothers.

"An older brother always tries to beat his younger brother at everything. For a time, this works. The older brother is always able to run faster and climb higher than the younger one. But one day the younger brother decides to get his revenge.

"'There is some fresh cow milk waiting at the top of that hill. Whoever gets to it first may drink it,' he says.

"Of course the older brother wants to be the fastest, so he runs and reaches the top of the hill first. Sure enough, when he gets there he sees a puddle of white liquid. Feeling pleased with himself, he puts his mouth down and drinks it in one gulp. He doesn't realize, until it is too late, that the white liquid is actually hyena dung. The younger brother is the one who has the last joke."

I must be better now for, although I am still weak and my sides hurt, I start to laugh. It is the image of the boy drinking dung that does it, especially since I can imagine playing a similar trick on my own brothers.

As I continue to recover, I lie on my mat and watch Mama perform her tasks around the house, as if I am a baby seeing her for the first time. I watch the solid upper muscle of her arm as she mashes groundnuts and prepares sorghum. I watch her pulling a tiny pink thread through coarse white cloth, "needling," the only time that she ever truly sits, as opposed to squatting when she is cooking or kneeling down when she serves my father his food.

I lie still and let Mama sing a lullaby to me, a song about a mother bringing her daughter fresh cow's milk.

The skin above Mama's nose crinkles when she smiles at

me, and yet there are times when I catch her with her smile off, as if she has forgotten to put it on. At these times, she looks like torn cloth.

I know Mama's biggest wish for me is that I follow a path different from her own, but at the same time, I want to sweep my house the way she does, always remembering to take the broom out of the hut and bang it against a tree to clean it off. I want my needling stitches to be tight and neat like hers. I want to cut vegetables as she does, so very thin, with the knife almost heading right into her thumb each time. Mostly I want to keep the faith the way she does, praying without fail two times a day.

My own prayers are rushed. I know I scatter my Blessed Gods about like careless stones, knowing that as soon as I have tossed enough of them, I may continue to play. Mama's prayers are slow and deliberate, placed just so, like her stitches.

"You don't take your prayers seriously, because life has been too good to you thus far," Mama scolds.

I suppose it is true. *Has life been good to you, Mama?*

I know Mama carries with her a cloak of sadness, which she takes on and off. When she is around me and the other children, she slaps her knee and laughs. She lets me rest my face on the back of her neck and breathe in the smoky scent of her braided hair.

But with my father, Mama is different — quiet, head low, hand in front of her mouth. This despite the fact that my father has attended school and does not choose to beat her.

"Still, I never went to school, so I must kneel." Mama shows me how rough her knees are. She makes me run my fingers across their crackly scars.

"Get an education. That way you will never have knees like mine. God saved you from malaria for a reason, Chi Chi."

I nod. I am hoping Mama will bring me tea with sugar, then tell me more stories. Instead she kicks my mat and says in a stern voice, "Get up now. It is time to go back to school."

"Go to school? Now? But I am still weak." During my illness I had Mama all to myself. I do not wish to give this up.

But Mama has made up her mind. "You must return to school. You have wasted too much time with illness already."

■■■

SEVERAL HARVESTS pass, and my brother Iko, who is one year older than me, turns fourteen. Mama must help him prepare for his initiation.

For this event, we make a huge bonfire. Iko has to jump over the fire while the elders give him thrashings with a black whip made of rhinoceros skin. Succeed, and he becomes a man. Fail, and he brings shame on our family.

Iko backs far away from the fire to get a running start.

"Jump!" I yell, so loud that the command cracks apart in my throat. Iko launches himself into the air with a holler. He clears the fire and lands on the ground with a thump. The elders sitting on the sidelines raise their gourds filled with home brew to show their approval.

Later, Iko lets me check his legs to see whether any of his leg hair got burnt off, but, no, it did not.

"You jumped so high," I say.

After the initiation, we girls cover our bodies with white paint and do a special dance. Because Iko was successful, I sing, "Oh, look at my brother, how handsome he is. I can't afford for someone to take my brother away." All of us girls dance, stomping our feet and shaking the beads and bells we have fastened to our ankles. Some of the men play dried gourds or lokembe, an instrument they play with their thumbs.

We girls curl our stomachs in and out and sway our bodies to the rhythm of the drums. We tease the boys, too, getting close to them and then bumping them away. When we dance like this and sing our private female songs, I think of all of us girls as being one, as being so happy and free that not even the earth's gravity can hold us down.

—4—

AFTER IKO'S INITIATION, we celebrate and dance. We eat goat meat and fresh blood drawn from the necks of cattle with miniature arrows.

The next morning I wake to a different type of blood.

"No, no. Not now." I look down and see droplets of blood forming red petals on the dirt.

I am furious. My stomach hurting me was what woke me out of my sleep, and now, standing up, I see blood — my first monthly womanhood — spilling onto the dirt.

At age thirteen, I am just a year older than Nadai was when she got married.

There are so few girls who are allowed to attend school as it is. Of these girls, several disappear from school each month because they do not have sanitary napkins. Instead of going to school, they go to their huts for days, constantly having to wash the cloths they keep between their legs. There is no place to change the cloths at school, our only bathroom being a not-so-private latrine pit behind the school that most of us never use since there are so many flies.

Now I wonder what I should do. Mama enters and, once

I tell her what has happened, she clicks her tongue, then goes and gets me a wad of spare cloth.

"You will not be a girl who misses school, not even for a day," she insists.

"Fine," I say with enough exasperation to let Mama know I am upset, but not enough to get me caned. It is not really Mama I am annoyed with. It is my own body.

I bundle the cloths Mama has given me as thickly as I can and stick them in my underwear. Then comes the walk to school, which I try to do without waddling like a duck.

As soon as I reach the classroom I sit down as quickly as I can and clamp my legs together, making sure the bloody cloths do not fall out. When the teacher asks us to stand and greet him, I do so with clenched legs. For the rest of the class I sit, thighs together, unmoving, legs going slowly numb. I focus on what the teacher is telling us. Some seasons ago, I annoyed the teacher, and my punishment was to dig a hole for the trash behind the school. Today I make sure that I do exactly as he says, lest I get sent on such a mission.

Despite my annoyance, it is good that I am at school, because on this day the teacher shows us a big yellowed map with all of the different continents. The map is so old and worn that part of Asia is torn away, but China remains, and our teacher points it out to us.

"China, a country that is quite interested in possessing some of our oil," he states. Our teacher is one of the few men I have ever seen wearing glasses, a gift from the missionaries. These glasses take up most of his face and make his eyes look huge. Also, he has a way of emphasizing each word when he speaks, as if each one is equally and extraordinarily important.

Next he points to the United Kingdom — "Home of the British who, along with Egypt, first colonized us."

The teacher pauses when he gets to North America. "This is where most of the English in the world is spoken," he explains. He tells us that the land in the United States is varied. Some of it mountainous, some of it flat as slate. Many different regions — north, south, east, west. He points to the Rocky Mountains in the western United States, "Tall like the Didinga Hills." Then, as an aside, he adds, "I once met a Baptist American missionary from the land of Tennessee, and he told me that all Americans love something called pro wrestling. These men dress in gold and silver and capes, then fight one another."

"Do they fight over land?" Tihou asks. She always asks good questions.

"I believe the wrestling matches are used to prove who is the most powerful."

Our boys wrestle — it is one of their favorite pastimes — but dressing up in gold and silver? This sounds strange, but fascinating.

Finally, the school day is over. As I walk home, I can feel the weight of the blood-soaked rags I am carrying inside my skirt. I pass by the enormous baobab trees, many of their branches knotted like the limbs of elders. The trees themselves seem to say, "We, too, have to fight to keep our limbs from dragging to the ground."

Tonight I will have to do extra washings, walk to the river when it is getting dark, plunge my hands into that cold water and scrub my skirt against a rock to remove the blood. When I dress in the morning, the uniform will remain wet, yet this is not too great a hardship. What is important is that I have proven I can be one of those girls who stays at school no matter what.

Still, I hate my body's change. Will the boys now start to bother me, to pay me notice? I think of my mother's friend Chocho hiding in the bushes, her face covered with leaves. I think of Nadai. My palms begin to tingle just as they did when I slapped my brother.

I will fight off any boy who bothers me, I promise myself, and I will do it with my own two hands if need be. Just try to touch me, I almost dare the boys. Touch me and watch how your fingertips will burn.

—5—

THOUGH ADULTS DO NOT discuss what goes on with a man and woman in the privacy of their huts, all of us girls know about what the adults do at night. We also know about babies. Most of us have seen our mothers pregnant and giving birth many times over. That is how women's lives are. Children on top of children.

On a day when the ground has begun to crack from dryness, Mama — who is pregnant again — doubles over herself with labor pains. On this very same day, my brother Lotiki's leg — achy and swollen since the beginning of the week — suddenly erupts into such pain that he runs for the small jug of water we keep in the hut and douses his leg with it. The water immediately reacts with the skin, puckering into an angry sore.

Upon further inspection, my brother sees a small white tail sticking out of this new wound. Guinea worm.

One of the town midwives ushers Mama into our third hut — the one that doubles as a birthing hut for all my father's wives — while a medicine man lays my brother on his back. The man takes a small stick which he uses to push on the bottom of my brother's wound, coaxing that worm out of its warm home in my brother's flesh. He says "Come, come" to the worm, as if he is talking to a small child. Next he wraps the worm around the twig as though threading a spool.

"Please, yank it out!" I scream, not wanting to see this worm in my brother's leg anymore.

"No, no. Pull the worm too quickly, and snap," he says, demonstrating how it can break into two pieces with the one piece still stuck in the leg. Instead he pulls a bit of the worm out and twists it around the stick. This pull and twist, pull and twist, just a little at a time, will continue for weeks, even months.

Releasing the worm from his body is a painful, slow birthing process. I watch to see if my brother cries out, thinking I can some day insult him by calling him a woman, but he does not. Rather, he clenches his lips together so tightly that it looks as though he has one lip instead of two.

They say the Guinea worm is clever. It begins as a tiny larva inside a flea, a mere speck of a thing. Once swallowed through dirty drinking water, it grows quietly inside its host, never causing a fuss, like a third wife. But there reaches a time when it wants to see the world, and it peeks out of the skin.

This is what happens with my brother. He hobbles around for weeks with a stick hanging out of his leg. The live creature is coiled around it.

Releasing a worm from my brother's body takes longer than releasing a baby from my mother's. Having given birth many times before, three times to live babies and many times to dead ones, Mama is accustomed to the bearing down it takes to push a baby out of her. Still, this does not stop her from shaking her head from side to side, as if disbelieving the pain.

I watch as the midwife with the skinny fingers massages Mama's belly with sesame oil as a way of feeling how the baby is positioned. She holds a compress made from boiled leaves to Mama's back to relieve some of the pressure and tries to get her to eat some porridge.

I do not like seeing Mama in so much pain. Her eyes squeezed shut, her neck bent, her body as stiff and crooked as a branch. What if I lose her? But Mama desperately hangs onto her life and that of the baby. I hear her praying between jagged breaths.

Once the baby is out, Mama fights to find the small bit of oxygen in the stifling hot hut. The tang of birth blood fills the room. With the help of the midwife, Mama tilts her pelvis to stem the bleeding. Then she takes the product of her labor, the new small life — a little girl — and puts her to her breast.

When she is done feeding her, Mama holds the baby up so I can see.

"Here it is," Mama says, holding my wrinkly, wet sister. To give her a name this early would be tempting the fates.

We have a saying, "You can't have a swaddling cloth before a baby is born, because until you see the baby, you do not know if it will be human or not." Our mothers lose so many babies that we do not count on this baby living until a few days have passed.

I look at my baby sister every day, stare at the crusty stump of her umbilical cord and run my fingers across the tight oily hair on her head.

Sometimes I whisper warnings into her tiny ears, the same ones Mama taught me. "Keep away from mosquitoes and puddles. Don't miss a day of school, not even one."

One morning I find the baby's umbilical cord lying beside her, curled up like a crinkly peanut.

"Mama!" I call out.

Mama inspects the dried-up cord, squeezes it between her fingers.

"Now your sister is a person," she says.

The naming ceremony takes place a few days later. Names come from families, local people and the Catholic church. That is why we have so many. One person may give you a name, but another may choose to call you by a different one. Names get strung together like links on a chain.

We name my sister Achii Iyom Ikaa Arminya. Achii is because she was born during thirsty times. Poor girl. If she had just waited a few more days to be born, she would have been named for the rain that followed — rain that was coaxed out of the sky by the elders.

The elders' magic is hard to explain. I do not know what goes on at their meetings where they discuss, among other things, the problem of no rain. My father once explained that they slaughter a goat and spread its entrails out so that they can interpret them. They then discuss whatever disharmony is preventing the sky from releasing water. They talk and talk, and when they are done, the sky lets forth a torrent of rain.

Oh, Achii, I wish you were named for the rain that bleeds along the ground, turning it dark and bringing out the bright color of the leaves. Instead, when people hear your name, their skin will crack and their throats will croak with the memory of dry days.

I hold my baby sister during those brief moments when she is not strapped to Mama's back, stick my face right over hers as she is lying on top of a goat skin. When I place my finger in her mouth, I am amazed at how strong her suck is. Achii is only a week old and yet, oh Lord, the will to survive and eat is so strong.

Forty days after Achii is born, we hold a big ceremony for her. All the villagers gather around. It is at this time that people give their unique blessings to the baby.

Nakiru, who is known for her ability to sew a dress after having measured you only with her eyes, says, "May you make your home peaceful."

One of the elders, Lomura, whose purplish lips are in a constant pucker and who, it is rumored, can hold his breath indefinitely underwater, says, "Achii, may you bring a good name to your family."

Finally, my father adds his own wish. "That your life should be a smooth one."

As Achii grows, the villagers will watch to see which of their blessings comes true. If she is successful in life, they will take credit for it.

—6—

A YEAR LATER, AS Achii is learning to take her first wobbly steps, soldiers begin to surround our village. They mill about, lean up against posts, their eyes scanning the horizon. There have always been soldiers, but now there are more of them, and they are restless, like animals sensing an oncoming storm.

I have grown so much that my school uniform — a white blouse and dark-blue pinafore — no longer fits me. Mama must buy me a new one, so she brews merti, our local beer, in order to earn some money.

I go with her because I have no choice, but also because I love the damp yeasty scent of brewing beer.

Mama has already soaked the cornmeal, allowing it to ferment. At the same time the sorghum has started to sprout.

"Roots!" I proclaim. This means the sorghum is ready to be boiled into porridge with the cornmeal. Soon it will be a sour fermented liquid, ready to drink.

Outside our hut, the soldiers from our Sudan People's Liberation Army stand in groups and bump shoulders with one another. Tensions between the North and South are worsening, fermenting just like our beer. We of the South want to practice our Christianity, whereas those of the North want to spread sharia. For us, we consider sharia law to be a poisonous weed.

How will we protect ourselves against the North? Though we have guns, they have missiles. We hold twigs while they hold tree trunks.

The soldiers buy the beer from Mama and drink it warm. I hand a cup to one of them before Mama quickly pulls me aside.

"These same soldiers who give us money are the ones who, if they drink too much alcohol, might turn around and violate us later on. Sell them the beer, but remain wary of them," she tells me in a low voice. "Always look at the eyes, Poni. If their eyes look cloudy from beer, that might mean trouble."

"Why don't you make changaa?" I ask Mama. "You'd earn more money." This alcohol made from palm sugar and yeast is a strong, pure alcohol.

"No. Never," Mama says. "There is good reason for people to call it kill-me-quick liquor. If it doesn't kill you, it might blind you. More money is one thing, but remember what they say. The higher the monkey climbs, the more danger he faces."

■ ■ ■

MY COUSIN KEIJI braids my hair in the sunshine. Keiji is all smiles, but her fingers are harsh and unforgiving, pulling my hair so hard that I feel every nerve ending in my scalp and tears forming in the corners of my eyes.

"Slow down! Stop hurting me," I tell her.

"And then what? We will be here until the sun disappears, eh?" When Keiji finishes, she has me feel the neat rows she has made.

She also pulls a letter from her dress pocket. "Here is the reward for your beauty. It's from a boy," she laughs. Keiji has the giggle of a fluttering butterfly.

I unfold it. It is from Akileo. They say that this boy, along with two of his friends, killed a lion. Not only that, but Akileo is tall with broad shoulders and legs whose muscles stand out in ridges against his calves.

I know I am supposed to be happy to receive a letter from one so fine and courageous. Certainly Keiji is hopping up and down with excitement. But all I feel is anger.

"What are you going to do?" Keiji asks.

I hesitate only for a moment. "I will go beat him, of course."

"It is a wonder any of the boys bother with you," Keiji calls after me, but I ignore her.

Later that afternoon, I march over to where Akileo is tending cattle. He is standing, brushing his teeth with a tree root, surrounded by the cows with their enormous horns.

I draw myself up as tall as I can. Even so, I only reach Akileo's chest.

"Did you write this?" I wave the letter in his face.

"I did," he says with a smile that reveals one front tooth, cocked just so, as though it is teasing me.

"I am not some lion you can hunt," I say, and I slap him as hard as I can across the chest. His chest feels thick as wood, and his skin makes a hollow *thuck* sound when I hit it. "If we married, you could hit me back," I tell him. "But we won't, not ever." And with that, I hit him again across the shoulder.

At this point he turns his body away from me and says, "Are you crazy?" Now he has tightened his lips, no longer flashing that tipped-to-the-side tooth at me.

"Stay off me," is all I say and turn on my heels.

■ ■ ■

A MONTH GOES BY and I do not hear from Akileo again.

"Thanks to God," I murmur to myself. The problem is that once word of this first boy's letter gets out, the other boys start to compete over me. My disinterest in boys makes me more interesting to them. They are like flies drawn to a cow's swishing tail.

A week later, as I am studying, Keiji approaches with another letter.

"Tell me this is not from Akileo," I groan.

"No," she says, her eyes wide with mystery. "If you can believe it, it's from Lokure."

"Oh, no, no," I say. "That skinny boy?"

"He's not so bad. At least he's a top student."

"Yes, but he spends his time with his sister and mother more than with the other boys."

Lokure's mother gave birth to nine infants, all of whom died except for his sister and him. Lokure's mother breast-fed him until he was old enough to climb trees, a fact which earned him mockery around the village.

When I go searching for Lokure, I find his sister Lele instead. I am surprised she is alone, since she usually follows Lokure wherever he goes.

"Where is your brother?"

"He is studying near our hut," she says.

I march straight over to Lokure. When he sees me, he lifts his hand up in greeting. I respond by shouting insults right into his face.

"Ugly," I tell him. "Your face is a thorn to my eye. Don't even look my way or I shall pierce you with a stick."

I do feel sorry for Lokure, the way his smile falls off and his chest caves in. But I don't apologize.

As I walk home, arms folded across my chest, blood pulsing within my cheeks, I am so distracted with my thoughts that I nearly run into a gazelle. It looks at me, and I stare right back, but it doesn't run. I scare everyone else off. Why not it?

Maybe the gazelle is waiting for me to explain myself.

"I had to be cruel to Lokure. Otherwise he might try to claim me."

The gazelle looks at me, its mouth full of grass, but its eyes sympathetic.

"I have to fight people off, you see," I continue. It has something to do with Nadai, with the image I have of her hanging from a rope. I imagine her disappointment when she saw the men coming for her. They cut her down then sent her right back to her husband.

As I walk away from the gazelle, I let the tall grass scrape against my legs. I love grass like this, grass so high you can disappear into it.

—7—

A WHOLE MONTH GOES BY, and Lokure doesn't contact me. Good, I think. But then, in a few weeks' time, one of his friends approaches me with another love letter from him.

Oh, tell me this is not so. Were my words not cruel enough? Does he think I have time to wind him out slowly, like the medicine man who lured the Guinea worm out of my brother's leg?

I don't. I long to yank him out and be done.

I call my male cousin Juma over. "Juma, please do me this one great favor. Find Lokure and beat him."

"I will," he says.

The next time I see Lokure on the way to school, he stares past me. I cannot see any marks on his face, but I presume, judging by his expression, that of a frightened bongo antelope, that my cousin thoroughly thrashed him.

Good. But then, after a few more weeks have passed, eyes be true, I see Lokure's friend trudging back towards me. In his hand, another letter.

"Am I crazy?" I ask. "Is this boy a poor dog begging for food scraps?" I take the letter and angrily put it in my skirt pocket. This time, I reason, I will go and beat Lokure myself, just as I did with Akileo.

I take the letter over to the small pile of trash we keep and burn every few days. I will set the fire right now. But, as I am about to put the letter in the trash pile, Lokure's looping handwriting catches my eye, and I begin to read the letter in spite of myself.

As I read, something goes soft inside me.

How to explain? There are words in this letter. Bold words that compare me to things of beauty — the arched branch of a tree, the gold of a sunset. I remember when Nadai and I held a mango in our hands and plunged our fingers into the sweet fruit, remember the gloriously sticky sensation. In his letter, Lokure tells me that I am like this fruit, sweet underneath a tough rind.

I have never seen writing as beautiful as this.

As I read Lokure's letter, my eyes begin to tear up. He is not supposed to know this side of me, the soft parts I have tried to cover with sticks.

I cannot, will not, let Lokure lure me in. He will not win me just because he is able to carve such beautiful images with his words. All boys seem sweet when they are trying to win the heart of a girl, but after marriage something changes. I know this. I saw how Chocho covered her cut-up face with leaves. I saw how Nadai's husband stole her light. I cannot allow Lokure's words, however magical, to pull me in.

Mama made it clear what marriage is like when she tugged on my hair and warned me about a life full of kneeling and beatings.

Yet, although it is my plan to do so, I cannot bear to burn

Lokure's letter. Instead I hide it in my pocket. I may need words such as these one day.

Then I go straight to Lokure. The slaps I rain upon his chest and across his face seem mechanical now. I hit him as though I am slashing away brush.

Lokure does not lift a hand to stop me. Instead he simply asks, "Do you not have a female's heart?" I do not answer his question, and I do not look back after I walk away.

A female's heart? It is quite possible that I do not. I run to Kinyeti and plunge my sore hands into her waters.

This river understands me. She is as cruel and cold as I am.

—8—

THERE ARE MORE BATTLES between the North and the South every day. Now there are soldiers everywhere in our village. Young boys tote around AK-47 guns. These boys seem so sure of themselves and their cause, but Mama shakes her head when she sees them.

At night, Mama talks with my oldest brother about the fighting taking place in the neighboring towns.

"We should run," Lotiki tells Mama. "The fighting will be here any day now. The government is getting weapons — bombs from China, even planes from Russia. They will make us swear allegiance with sharia and study only Arabic in our schools."

"Run?" Mama repeats, as if she hasn't heard him properly. "Where would we run to? Our home, our cattle, our goats, our chickens, our crops. Everything we have is here." She points to the ground. "This is our home, and this is where we stay."

■■■

ONE NIGHT, WHEN I AM supposed to be sleeping, I sit up

listening while my father makes time with Lokolong, the chief of a nearby village. The two men chew miraa, a bitter plant stem that enables them to stay up talking most of the night. Our sleeping and common room are separated only by a curtain, so I hear everything.

"I have a riddle for you," Lokolong says.

"Go ahead," my father urges.

"What is an African's biggest curse?"

"Tell me."

"The biggest curse is discovering valuable resources on your own soil."

"This is the truth." My father has small eyes but large, extra-round cheeks. I always imagine these cheeks to be pouches, used to store extra words inside, for my father is never at a loss for words. He is known throughout our village as a man who is able to see a single problem from many angles.

Lokolong continues, "Our natural riches will be our downfall. People have smelled oil, and now they will tear our land apart to get it."

"So what do we do? Leave? Negotiate?"

"Negotiate against the Northerners? They have the big weapons. The government is backing them up."

"True. The North will not be satisfied until it has eaten us whole, bones and all."

My father and his friend are traditional in the way they deal with problems. They have seen war, drought, cattle raids — so through talk, they can figure out what to do.

The sound of my father's voice makes me drowsy. My head is like a heavy fruit in my hand.

Finally, I lie down next to my sister on our sleeping mat.

She says my name, one of the new words she has learned, and I stroke her hair, which is almost long enough to be braided. The sound of her soft breathing, as she falls into sleep, gives me comfort.

—*9*—

THINGS DO NOT GET better in weeks to come. The SPLA
sets up a training camp right in Kapoeta, the town closest
to ours. They hang a big sign that says Red Army, and they
attempt to recruit all boys, young and old, waving them
over, holding up their guns this way and that so that the sun
glints off of them.

"What boy wishes to carry a gun?" they call out. "What
boy wishes to fight for the cause?"

Many of the boys are excited by the chance to have a fire-
arm. They secretly hope they will be able to keep it even
after the war is over. The new recruits march while they
sing:

> *Garang is coming.*
> *Serve the cause. Liberate the South.*

One day I am there in the market helping Mama sell her
beer. SPLA soldiers mill about.

I recognize one of them. His name is Lopwanya, and he
is my same age.

"How are you?" he asks.

"Fine," I respond, dropping my eyes. Lopwanya used to be undersized, but now he has sprouted upwards. Because of his height, his gun and his SPLA army uniform — dark green camouflage and topped by a red beret — I can tell he thinks himself very important.

Next to him is his younger brother, Amadeo, who also holds a gun.

"Poni, would you like to come and touch my gun?" Lopwanya asks, and all the other boys laugh.

Some of the boy soldiers have a crazy look in their eyes. Yet perhaps they are not drunk from beer. Can boys get drunk from carrying guns?

What I do know is that I don't trust them. The soldiers sing:

> *The army leads me.*
> *The army is my father now.*

"What do those songs mean?" I ask Mama later.

"John Garang tells these boys the gun is their new father. And what? This is supposed to make them forget their real fathers?"

I picture Lopwanya, holding his gun like a prized fish that he has speared. For him it is a treasure, this gun.

"The mothers work hard to birth these boys, and now they are trying to die young." Mama shakes her head. "They bring shame upon us."

Many of our people were happy to see the SPLA soldiers when they set up camp in Chukudum. They came, after all, to defend us against the government and against the North, but these days the soldiers hardly seem to be on our side. At first we gave these young men food whenever they asked for it, but since that time they have become more demanding.

"I would gladly give you food, but there's none left," my neighbor Akongo tells a soldier named Gai. He paces outside her door like a nervous leopard. He shakes his empty container in front of her.

"You need to fill this with grain. Show me you support the war efforts. Otherwise we will have to make things difficult for you."

Akongo puts her hands on her hips. "I am truly out of millet and corn."

I feel my own palms begin to tingle as I clench my hands into fists. Without thinking, I say, "Aren't you the same soldier who came and took her grain just a few days ago? How can you be so greedy?"

Gai stomps towards me and plunges the butt of his gun into the soft place in my stomach. It doesn't hurt so much as push the breath out of me.

"Keep quiet, little sister."

He turns back to Akongo. "You have left me no choice but to search this place." He calls over three other soldiers, and the four of them paw through everything she owns. They quickly become frustrated because, just as she told them, there is no food to be found.

"Give us your beads then," they say, pointing to some ceremonial beads they have found.

"Are we not on the same side of the fight?" she protests. "Are we not all Southerners?"

"I do not want to fire off my gun," the pacing-like-a-leopard soldier replies. "Don't force me to do it."

She hands over her beads. What soldiers will do with beads is anyone's guess, but perhaps, by stealing from her, they are not leaving empty-handed.

"A hungry soldier with a gun is a dangerous thing," Akongo mutters behind the soldiers' backs. She turns to me. "Really, you must learn to hold your tongue, Poni. Otherwise you'll get us all killed."

That night, as I am helping Mama cut up greens for our meal, a group of soldiers gathers around another neighbor, Mauro. Mauro himself is a member of the SPLA, but he is an older man, too old for fighting.

One of the soldiers points his gun at him. "Are you loyal to the SPLA?"

"Yes," Mauro replies.

"Why did you leave town and then come back?" they ask. "Are you an Arab?"

"Not an Arab, no. I moved to the bush because I was afraid our village would be attacked."

"So you fled rather than staying to fight?"

"I'm here now," he says. "Ready to help, ready to support the cause."

"You're ready to help, eh? Well, you can start now, then. Start by carrying this ammunition."

Mauro puts out his arms dutifully, but then the soldiers begin to load him down with heavy ammunition, so many big rifles and pieces of metal that he says, "This is getting too heavy."

"Are you refusing orders?" one of the soldiers asks in a mocking voice. "Maybe you're a traitor. Go on. Carry this ammunition, brother." He pushes Mauro forward.

Don't they see his arms shaking? Don't they see the

look of shame and pain on his face? By now women are coming out of their huts carrying their soup pots. Some of the men, who are returning from tending cows, also stop and watch. Is this some type of game the soldiers are playing with Mauro?

Mauro does try to carry the load. He takes a few steps, but then his knees collapse under the weight of the heavy metal. He falls down, pieces of ammunition clattering around him, and I realize with horror that one of the soldiers has shot him. Mauro makes a sound, "Eee." Then he is no longer moving, no longer making any noise.

"He is useless to us," one of the soldiers mutters and kicks dirt on his crumpled-up body. People are too shocked to speak. The soldier yells, "We expect you, our people, to be loyal to your army, to your liberators. Otherwise what will you do when the government comes to attack?"

Mama tries to cover my eyes, but I push her hand away. Mauro, alive moments ago, is now unmoving. And for what?

Now Mauro's first wife, Eunice, comes running out of the hut followed by several children who clutch at her skirt. She looks from the soldiers to her husband, then screams, "Why, God?" The children start pawing at her, but she pushes them away. "Go back inside!" The children stand there just looking at their father, whose blood is emptying onto the ground.

"Is he all right, Mama?" one of the little girls asks. At this the mother goes wild, swatting at that child, swinging her arms as if she is fighting off a swarm of locusts.

"Go far from here," she screams. This makes the children run back into the hut. They are wailing, and I see one of the girls pulling at her own hair as she runs.

Eunice turns to the soldiers and, making herself tall, she says, "What will God think of you? You will answer to him some day."

After the soldiers leave, Mama goes over to Eunice to comfort her, while the men carry Mauro's body away. I am still rooted to my spot, surrounded by scattered green kale leaves that were to be our meal.

Later, my brothers and Mama speak again.

"That killing. That was not Garang's doing. He wants to unite Sudan, not tear it apart," Lotiki says.

"Yes, but the SPLA hires these crazy young men," Mama replies.

"These boys walk all day carrying their own ammunition and food on their heads, and they start to go mad. They drink beer and take drugs, then they start firing off those guns like they are toys."

Mama just shakes her head. "How are these soldiers our liberators? They would kill us just like the Northerners."

Lotiki gets serious. "I tell you we need to leave. It is not safe here."

"Not without Baba," Mama says softly.

My father is with one of his other wives right now. Yet Mama cannot make big decisions without him. At this moment she looks helpless and limp-shouldered. I hate to see her look so weak.

−10−

THAT NIGHT, AS I LIE freshly bathed and wrapped in goat skins, I ask my mother, "If you had to live without eyes or ears, which would you choose?"

"You are like a chicken pecking at corn with all your questions. Go to sleep. Don't wake your sister."

"But which would you choose?"

"Chi Chi, you are going to use up all the questions in the world. Quiet yourself."

I stop talking, but in my head I continue to ask myself the questions. Would I rather lose my ability to see the purple-black sky or sing in the choir? Would I rather give up mangoes or dancing? I continue to go back and forth as if I am my father weighing a problem, looking at it from this way and that way. At some point, I drift into sleep.

But then, without warning, I am awake.

I run out of the hut with my hands over my head as if they can somehow shield me from whatever it is falling down upon me. When I look up, the first thing I notice is the moon, fat as a cow's belly, but what I see next are the planes and the bombs that are falling out of them. So many bombs. It is as though they are coming from everywhere at once, as though the sky is raining down black eggs.

Is the world ending? All around me people are screaming, and some people are falling down upon the ground. I
see Mama holding Achii, but I cannot get to her. I see Salva, one of the village musicians, fall down, blood pooling
out like black ink around him, his mouth gasping like a fish
out of water. I hear screams coming from all sides. Am I
one of those screaming? Were we not all of us asleep only
moments ago?

People are running in all directions, as if they are playing a football match with no ball and no rules. They bump
into one another. There are soldiers in camouflage jackets
running and ducking through the crowd, shouting things
I cannot hear and then disappearing from sight. Because it
is dark, I cannot even tell whose side these soldiers are on.
Enemy or friend? Government or SPLA?

"Run!" I hear Mama yell, and I do. My body springs into
action, leaving the falling-down bodies behind me. I run so
fast that I am convinced that my feet are no longer touching the earth but that they are treading air just above the
ground. I cannot hear any sounds outside of me, only the
sound of my own breathing, as though I am underwater.
In, out, in, out — so loud that I fear I might use every bit
of oxygen in the world.

Bombs are still falling. The earth is dancing with their
vibrations.

Then I am at Kinyeti River. Without thinking, I jump
in. The river is already filling up with people who reach
their arms out. The arms wave at me like some strange
water creature. Some of the arms are trying to help me,
while others are trying to pull me under. There is blood in

the water. The cold surrounds me and, just as I did when I was a child learning to swim, I struggle against the water. I can no longer tell which way is up and which way is down within the dark waves.

Suddenly, I am on someone's back. I have no idea who this man is that I am now riding. Only the top of his head is visible above the water. I cannot see his face, but I can feel his shoulder blades rising and falling like the wings of a bird. For a few brief moments, our bodies are one, every part of me pressed into every part of him. We are on top of the water, then below it. Water burns my nose, and I can barely breathe.

Abruptly, I am on the shore, on the other side of the river. I still do not see the face of the man who rescued me. He dives back into the water.

I keep running. There are men and women running near me. Each of us is running for his own life. From the corner of my eye, I look at the woman running across the field from me. She is carrying one child in front of her, a little girl who jostles up and down as she runs, and a baby on her back. Something makes me look twice at this baby, and when I do, oh, dear God, I suddenly feel as if I will not be able to run anymore. Every part of me goes numb.

This baby has no head. He must have been hit by a bomb. Here is his mother running, running, and she has no idea that this baby on her back no longer has any head on him.

Someone has to stop her. Someone has to take that baby from her.

Suddenly, as if guessing my thoughts, the woman reaches behind her. A scream, both of us at once, and then another bomb falls, sending her, along with the girl and the headless child, onto the ground in a heap. I am ill when I find myself actually thanking God for this death.

■■■

IT IS A WHOLE NIGHT and day before I stop running. Other survivors who have also been running gather into a group.

"We should go to Torit," someone says.

"No. They'll be attacked next," another replies.

One of the men says, "My cousin told me aid workers have set up a safe haven in Kakuma."

"But it is too far away."

"Far away is a good thing. We can walk to Narus, then over the border to Lokichoggio. We will be safe there."

We have nowhere else to go. I look around trying to locate Mama and my siblings. They are nowhere to be seen. There is nothing to do but walk with this new group.

Though our group survived the first round of bombs, we are not safe. We know that each bomb has brothers and sisters, that more bombs might fall on us at any time.

To stay hidden, we walk mainly at night, when the darkness can camouflage our blue-black skin, and when the air is cooler. I do not count our walk in miles but rather in days, and soon I lose track even of these. Day into day into day. This is how it goes. After weeks of nothing to eat but leaves and a few odd fruits, buzzards begin to circle around certain ones of us. Most people slowly move away from those who have been singled out by these birds.

■■■

THERE IS A SWAYBACKED boy — I do not know his name — whom I am often walking near. I can tell that up until now, this little boy was standoffish, the type of rebellious boy that I like. Unlike many of the children who do not complain but who simply turn listless, he seems annoyed by his slow starvation. As days go by, this boy loses the last bit of roundness in his cheeks.

"I wish I could still spit," he tells me.

The one thing he can still do is jut out his jaw in defiance, a jaw that seems to get sharper as the rest of his face and body thins. After a while he is all bones, stomach and eyes — two bulging eyes that begin to lose their light.

"Hop onto my back," I tell him. He alights on me as though he is a small bird. I feel him rest his cheek on my back. Though we have only recently met, we have known each other forever. His breath is so quiet near my ear, and it gives off an odor that is sweet, but like rotting fruit.

Despite the fact that he is so light on my back — a bundle of sticks — I am weak enough that even this feels like too much after a whole day of walking. The boy senses this.

"Put me down."

I do. We sit together, his eyes, yellowy orbs, fixated on my face. He no longer looks like a boy. He looks like a tiny, very old man.

"Sing to me," he commands. Though I never prayed as well as Mama, when I sang in choir, I could send my voice straight up to God. Now my voice is dry, stuck inside my throat. Singing loudly takes too much effort.

Never mind. This situation calls for a very soft song. I sing the song my brother used to sing to his bull:

I love my white bull,
His coat so smooth and white.

"Do you see those buzzards overhead?" the boy asks me. "Perhaps there is food nearby. Maybe that buzzard has spotted some meat."

I cannot tell him the truth about the buzzards, the real reason they have come.

"Yes, we will eat meat soon," I tell him, and he juts out his jaw and smiles ever so slightly. The corners of his mouth are oozing white liquid.

"Can you walk some more, boy?" I ask.

He glares at me. "No. I will stay here. Your song has made me too sleepy. I will just close my eyes for a while. I want to be rested when we find that meat."

A few hours later, as evening starts to fall, all of us get up to start walking again, but the standoffish boy does not.

His death does not match his personality. Like my song, it is too quiet. I walk away from him and do not look back. I do not want to see the gloat in the buzzard's eye, that look of I-told-you-so.

—11—

"WHEN WE GET TO Kakuma, there will be food. In Kakuma we will be safe. The others will be there in Kakuma, waiting for us." People repeat these phrases to one another like refrains. When my throat becomes too dry to speak aloud, I repeat these phrases inside my head.

This is what keeps me going. I dream of Mama's hot fish stew, of sleeping with Achii on our mat. I think of swimming in Kinyeti, of my brothers laughing.

At one point we see a group of Didinga people traveling by Land Rover. I am so jealous of them. The Land Rover moves slowly, owing to the fact that there are far too many people piled inside — people hanging out the windows, people on top of people.

Still, we call out to them, "Eh, eh, add me! Give me a lift! I will stand on someone's head!" We are not trying to be comical.

The soles of my feet are burnt from the hot earth. I am wearing sandals made from tires, but they are so worn that I can feel the skin of my feet burning away and thorns poking through. These dreadful feet of mine are constantly paining me, and yet I am beholden to them.

The white Land Rover passes us by without stopping. I am too numb to feel sad. I simply command my feet to keep walking.

The next day we overtake the remains of this Land Rover. Though the vehicle is intact, there are dead people and body parts everywhere.

"A land mine," people say.

Maybe some individuals got away. But, from the looks of it, this is highly unlikely. So many people killed in one quick explosion. In my head I add to the list of dangers — starvation, soldiers, bombs — hidden mines which, at any step, might kill me instantly.

■ ■ ■

IN THE BEGINNING, my stomach speaks to me, begs me for food. It becomes its own demanding person.

Here is what I know. When the body is not given enough food it will begin to eat itself up. In fact I can feel my own body chewing at my insides. But then, after a few days I stop feeling this constant pain. Instead I feel lighter.

Suddenly, it is easier to walk, because there is less of my body to move forward. Dizziness allows me to float along the ground, to glide. I begin to view myself as though I'm outside my body. But then, just as I think I have managed to ignore my hunger for good, it takes hold of me yet again, grabs me and shakes me. *You didn't think you could forget about me.*

At that moment I know I will eat anything I can find. And I do — leaves, insects, even some grass. At one point I find a snake and eat it raw with its skin still on. When I swallow, I feel the snake's scales rough against my throat. I eat, and then, a few hours later, I have to walk bent forward like a very old person, because the stomach cramps are so great. When the diarrhea hits, I simply do as the others do and squat right where I am standing. Leave the group in an attempt to find privacy, and you risk being left behind or eaten by a lion.

Too much diarrhea can mean death. I know this. I keep my hands on my stomach as if I can hold all the things I have eaten inside of me. I will everything to stay inside of me. Don't pour out of me. I command my body to digest the leaves and grass I have put into it. When I feel my throat gagging or my stomach clenching, I force these muscles to relax.

Weeks go by. As we walk, people sometimes fall down dead. As for me, my mouth gets so dry that my tongue splits down the middle. Though it still hangs inside my mouth, it is useless. I can do nothing with it. Part of me wishes I could remove it completely.

I remember Mama telling me that I was going to use up all the questions in the world. Maybe this has, in fact, come to pass. Maybe I will forever be speechless.

■ ■ ■

TIME NO LONGER PASSES in weeks but in shuffling footsteps. It takes food to make your body work. This is a simple fact. With hardly any food inside me, my thoughts spin in very slow circles. Sometimes I can manage nothing more complicated than the idea that I must continue to put one foot in front of the other.

My legs become swollen and filled with fluid. They constantly give me pain, but then, at one point, this pain stops. Though the lack of pain is a welcome relief, I know it is a bad sign, that my legs are slowly going dead. I keep walking, even though I have no feeling left below my waist.

I am no longer aware of the group of people around me. Instead I think about the people I have left behind. I think of Mama and my father but other people also flit in and out of my consciousness. My teacher with his huge glasses. Salva, who used to make such lovely music.

And then, unexpectedly, I find myself thinking of Lokure, the skinny boy who wrote me the love letters. It seems so very long ago that I held that last letter in my hand, stuck it in my pocket rather than burning it. Remind me, why exactly did Lokure write to me? Ah, yes. He wrote because he thought me beautiful. I nearly laugh at this thought. From what I can see of myself, my legs are swollen, my feet burnt and poked through with thorns. I have missing toenails. Even my hair has gone yellow.

Beautiful, ha!

Lokure is surely dead, dead like so many others. Maybe knowing this allows me to admit something. He was sweet, that boy. True, I didn't think him sweet while he was pestering me with his letters. Nor did I think him sweet when I was beating him up. But for whatever reason, I think it now.

As I continue to walk, I begin to have imaginary conversations with him.

"Lokure, you really thought I was beautiful once? Is this true?"

"Of course. Didn't I tell you so in my letter?"

"*You did.*"

"*Ah! I caught you. So you read my letter after all.*"

"*I meant to burn it, but your words... Well, I might as well confess that I liked your words very much.*"

"*I see. So having your cousin beat me and then beating me yourself was your way of thanking me?*"

"*I had to do it. Maybe if I see you again in this life or the next, I'll be able to explain it to you. In the meantime, can I assume that you regret having written me?*"

"*I regret nothing. You are beautiful, Poni. I stand by my words.*"

"*You're mocking me. Look at me now. My tongue is so dry that it is like a dead lizard in my mouth. In a matter of weeks, I have turned into an old woman. Back when you knew me, I didn't want to be beautiful, didn't want you to notice me.*"

"*But now?*"

"*Now I am just so hungry. I am hungry for food, but I am also hungry for words. I wish I could hear more of your beautiful words.*"

■ ■ ■

FOR DAYS, I CONTINUE to have silent conversations with Lokure and with other people I can no longer see. The conversations I have in my head don't require the use of a real tongue.

Mostly, I speak to Mama.

"*Mama, I wish I could smell your braids once more, put my head on your neck. When I ran, I didn't realize I would lose you.*"

■ ■ ■

SWEET JESUS. I have accepted the fact that no one is coming to save me or offer me a ride. I keep walking on my tattered feet towards Kakuma. This place is no longer real. Only a word, a hope.

At one point, our group finds a small puddle of water. One of the men touches it with his finger to make sure it is not a mirage. I do not bother about the flies, mosquitoes or the mud. Without hesitating, I move my face close and drink. Together, as a group, we suck that puddle dry. We bump heads as we try, all of us, to place our lips in the sludge. Mud fills my mouth like blood.

This bit of water makes my tongue burn, a sign that it has not died completely, yet my tongue still hangs in pieces inside my mouth, cut-up ribbons.

As we walk, I look to the moon. Like me, she is losing her roundness. She is growing smaller and smaller each day. Soon she will disappear altogether.

■ ■ ■

THEN ONE DAY, JUST like that, our walk is finished. We have reached Lokichoggio. None of us cheers or celebrates. In Lokichoggio the police receive us and assign us to white United Nations Land Cruisers that will transport us across the desert to Kakuma, the refugee camp where we have been promised safety. We obediently pack ourselves into these vans, our bodies pressed up against one another, bone against bone, and from there we ride to the refugee camp.

I feel no joy as we approach the barbed-wire fences. My eyes are so stiff that they can barely move back and forth. The sights around me come into focus slowly, and when they do, I am filled with a dull disappointment.

Perhaps my eyes have not yet cleared, but why does Kakuma look so dry and so brown?

—*12*—

INSIDE THE CAMP, the foolishness of my hopes is revealed. Did I really believe I would find paradise here? A place filled with mangoes and streams in the middle of the desert? I should have taken my lesson from the Bible. God punishes, not rewards, those who hunger for fruit.

I do not know what I was expecting from Kakuma, but certainly not this. Not thousands upon thousands of displaced people. Not a dust bowl that passes as a camp.

Kakuma is as far from salvation as one could imagine. In fact, the minute I enter the camp, the wind hits, stirring up a dust storm that stings my cheeks and eyes. I am sure that my eyes would be watering were it not for the fact that I am out of everything wet — saliva, sweat, mucus, blood — anything liquid that my body might have once produced.

We are given small cups of water, and I gently prod my tongue with my dirty fingers. My tongue is rutted and torn just like the bottoms of my feet, but I think it may mend.

The first security guard I see is a Kenyan man. He tells me his name, Kamau, and points to his guard's uniform. I have a great deal of difficulty talking because of my damaged tongue, but I manage to slur out my name as though I have consumed too much of Mama's home brew. Kamau fills out some paperwork, then hands me a card.

"This is your identification and ration card," he explains. "Don't lose this. Otherwise there will be no food or water for you."

I take the card in my hand, but where should I put it? I have only a tattered skirt with no pockets, and I am wearing only half a blouse.

How did I lose most of my skirt? It takes me a moment to remember. Then I do. I used part of it to make a bandage for a girl who got bitten by a scorpion during the trek. I do not remember her name, that one, but she was a girl who was always talking to herself. Our group was sitting and resting when she got bitten. I heard a clicking noise, then saw the scorpion scoot away.

As quickly as I could, I bound this girl's leg. It did no good. First her eyes began to bulge. I was really frightened that they might fall out. Then her tongue became swollen until it filled her entire mouth, and she was writhing on the ground, unable to breathe.

Her death was not peaceful like that of the standoffish boy who went quietly. No. I could do nothing to assist this girl. All I could do was watch as her face went green.

I look at the card Kamau has given me and quickly memorize the number on it. From now this will be me, a number. Next, I am given two misshapen metal cups — one filled with dried maize, the other with cooking oil.

"Your food ration." The guard adds, "We are low on food, so do what you can to stretch these bits. They will need to last a few weeks." I nod, though really, how can one stretch grains? He might have well asked me to squeeze water from a stone.

"When does this get refilled?" I ask.

"Sometimes the food arrives within a couple of days, sometimes a week. When it is time to queue for new food, you must reach there very early and hold your place in line, because sometimes the supplies do not last."

The security guard asks me if I traveled to the camp with anyone.

"I don't know where my family is."

"How old are you?"

"Fifteen."

"So you will be given the label of an unaccompanied minor. You will be assigned a foster family." Kamau takes hold of a woman who is standing nearby. "Loriho." He reads her name from the paper she is holding. "Where are your children, Mama?" he asks the woman in a loud, deliberate voice.

"God has taken them," she replies.

"This one here," he points to me. "She is Poni. She will now be your foster daughter."

The woman and I eye each other suspiciously for a few moments. Loriho does not say anything, just nods in my direction. I understand that I am to go with her.

She walks stiffly. Mama always had a sway to her walk. Unlike Mama, I can tell that this Loriho, even on her best days, never laughed so hard that she had to press her fingers into the corners of her eyes.

I cannot make sense of all this. One day I was living in my village with my family, and now?

I long for my mother with the deepest of aches. I would

give anything, even go through another round of malaria, just to have her with me again, just to watch her cut up onions, hear her laugh.

Though I have come all this way on my own, it is too dangerous to be unattached in the camps. A young girl alone might be grabbed. And so I stay with this new woman.

My foster mother doesn't look capable of taking care of herself, much less anyone else, so how much protection can she actually give me? She, too, has lost her entire family. In this sense, we are connected, though this is the only thing I admit to having in common with her.

If I knew that running so far and so fast would mean I would not see Mama again, would I still have run? It was so hard to see on the night the bombs fell on our village, so hard to hear. I have images from those terrible moments, but I cannot seem to put them in the correct order.

What of you, Baba? Were you able to talk your way out of whatever bad situation you met? Did you use all of those extra words you kept stored inside your cheeks? And my brothers, so strong, so capable. Were you able to jump your way to safety? Jump straight up into the sky?

■ ■ ■

WEEKS PASS. BACK HOME we grew what we needed. The plants practically pushed themselves out of the ground. The joke was, plant a Coke bottle, and you'll get an onion.

Here in Kakuma, nothing grows. I should feel gratitude that I am safe, that I am alive, and surely I do, but I cannot help complaining. "Why did I walk all this way only to end in such a dry place?"

When I first arrived, I thought I would only stay for a brief time, would find my family and return to my village. But then I learned the truth. I found out that my village was completely destroyed during the attacks, was burnt to the ground. Knowing this makes something turn hard as clay within me.

On the walk to Kakuma, my body nearly died. Now it is my spirit that I worry about.

—*13*—

THE GROUND HERE IS as cracked and gray as an elephant's skin. Time barely moves.

I am always waiting. I wait for rations, wait for the guards to split open the big white bags of donated grains. Yet I am secretly waiting for something more miraculous. For the skies to split open and rain meat and bread down upon us, as happens in the Bible. And I beg you, Lord, if it is not too much trouble, might I request some greens to go along with this meat and bread? Greens like we used to grow back home — chards, kales, collards and sukamawiki.

In this land of nothingness, there are no trees to sit under, and the only shade is that which our shadows provide.

Inside the camp I see so many too-thin children. Hunger comes and grabs each morsel of flesh that it can find. Some of the children no longer have any buttocks, the last bit of flesh to go. They can no longer sit comfortably since there is nothing to protect their small tailbones. So they lie sideways, lie on mats near their mothers, or sometimes on the ground itself. Some of them are so still that I can barely see them breathe.

I see a woman who looks old enough to be a grandmother, and yet she is offering a thin, droopy breast to a child. This child looks up at her with dead-cow eyes. He will not make it to the day's end.

I get used to seeing sights like these. Yet the stranger thing is how life goes on. There are football matches. There is a boy — I don't know his name — but every time he sees me, he does a little dance.

Life goes on, because it must. I help my foster mother erect a shelter with a piece of corrugated tin and a few chunks of wood. Both of us are short enough that we have to stand on the tops of our toes to hoist the piece of metal up. The shelter is nothing more than sticks covered by a bent piece of metal, yet it offers a small amount of protection. My foster mother spends all of her time under this shelter. She has no energy for activities other than squatting and swatting at flies. When there is grain to grind, she does it, but she does not find time to gossip or visit, as many of the other women do. She is merely passing her days.

However, she does seem to muster the energy to order me about.

"Poni," she calls sharply to me.

"Auntie?" I cannot bring myself to call her Mama.

"Go and fetch firewood."

"Yes," I reply. Had it been my own mother who had asked, my feet would have flown. But my true mother is not here.

I begin to walk and, as I do, I see a small group of girls who have been sent on this same collecting mission. We regard each other warily, realizing that we will be competing over the scarce wood. I see the girls start to walk away from me, but then one of them seems to change her mind.

"There is safety in numbers," she says. "Follow us." We walk together, not so close as to speak to one another. Our eyes sweep back and forth, looking out for either wood or danger.

After walking for a time, we hear footsteps behind us.

"Turkana!" one of the girls cries out.

She need only utter this one word before all of us are running. The Turkana are nomadic herders, lawless and dangerous.

I run out ahead of the others. I see one of the girls trip behind me, the same girl who told me to follow her.

When a lion chases a pack of antelopes, all of them scatter except for the one the lion seizes and pulls down. This girl is that unlucky antelope. A man is on top of her.

I run and hide inside a prickly thorn bush. Then I put my hand over my own mouth to stifle the urge I have to cough and scream. The man's blue-and-red-checked blanket falls over the girl like a net. I hear the man's grunts, see him moving up and down like an animal devouring its prey, and then he is gone.

I want to go to the girl, but there is nothing I can do to help her now.

The girl doesn't cry. Her legs wobble as she tries to stand, and she looks dazed. But she does get up. She gets up and, after wiping herself off, starts to look for firewood. She still needs that wood.

I know what will happen to her. She will be blamed for her own rape. No one will want to marry her, and people will call her malaya, a prostitute.

I wait until the girl is gone before I come out of the bush and begin looking for my own sticks.

Of course it could have been me who tripped, me who got caught. Yet I also know my fast running saved me. "You were born running," my mother used to say. The women around the village used to laugh to see me run.

■ ■ ■

I RETURN TO LORIHO later that evening carrying a few thin sticks. Despite the fact that my skin is already cut and my lip is torn from hiding in the thorny bush, Loriho takes an acacia branch and beats me across the shoulders.

"What took you so long?" she demands. It is not like when Mama used to beat me and would give me tea and sugar afterwards, her secret way of telling me that I was still loved. This woman continues to give me a sharp eye even after she is done with her caning.

That night, as I am sleeping, I wake suddenly to find my foster mother standing over me. I suck in my breath. She cannot possibly want to beat me at this time of night, can she?

Instead she kneels down next to me. Her eyes are unfocused, making me wonder if something is wrong with her. My heart is pumping hard, and I am too afraid to let her know that I am awake, so I lie there, eyelids fluttering.

"Nakang, daughter of mine," my foster mother says. She sucks on her fingers, then runs them over my face. "I am wiping tears from your face, Nakang."

Nakang? My foster mother, walking in her sleep, must think I am the daughter she lost. Am I the daughter's same age? Despite the fact that I have no fondness for my foster mother, I cannot help pitying her. Though it disgusts me, I allow her to trail her wet fingers over my face.

Let her believe, just for the night, that this daughter is still alive.

The next day, my foster mother seems to have no memory of her nighttime activities. Before sending me out for water, she tells me, "You will soon be married to a man here in Kakuma. I will find someone who can offer a bride price."

I turn my head away from her so she cannot see the burning in my eyes.

I will beat anyone who tries to claim me as a wife. I have done it before.

—14—

AT FIRST I LOOK FOR my family constantly. I look everywhere. My eyes never stop searching. But I lose a bit of hope every day, until gradually, I am left with nothing, only a carved-out spot inside of me. I get to where I no longer expect to see anyone, to where I barely raise my head.

Perhaps this is why, when I look up one day and see Lokure standing before me, I think he must be a ghost. My whole body begins to tremble.

"Poni, is it you?" he asks, as if he, too, cannot believe it.

"It is me," I say. How can I explain that I am me but not me, that I am a completely different version of the girl he once knew?

I recall a time when I shouted insults straight into Lokure's face: "Skinny! Ugly!" Now I can only imagine how I must appear to him, my hair yellowed, my body that of a dried-out lemon.

Seeing Lokure fills me with too many emotions at once. I am relieved that he is alive, more relieved than I care to admit. Yet I am also filled with embarrassment, as if I should confess all the imaginary conversations I had with him inside my head.

I want to confess everything to him. I want to tell him that back when I was walking those hundreds of miles across the desert, I watched an old woman die sitting up. Our group had stopped in order to let this woman rest. She died clutching a crust of bread someone had thrust upon her in the hopes that this small bit of sustenance might prevent her death. No one else noticed her die. The line between barely alive and barely dead was as tiny as a breath itself.

Nor did anyone see how I crept over to her, then took the bread out of her hands and put it into my own mouth.

I remember how the bread tasted, like tears.

How can I explain to Lokure that the love letter he wrote me so long ago, along with the bread out of a just-dead woman's hands, helped me survive days and nights of shuffling across the desert? Lokure's words replaced the other ones that kept pounding through my head, the ones that told me to just lie down and let death brush over me like sand.

Lokure's words were what kept me on my feet. Somehow his words kept me from thinking about the fact that my feet no longer had skin on the bottom or that my tongue was so torn that I might never use it again. They reminded me that somewhere there was still beauty to be found.

I want to tell everything to Lokure, to have him absolve me, but perhaps he has his own cross to bear. After all, how did he manage to walk all this way on those stick-skinny legs of his?

I remember when I beat him. Now I want to do the opposite, to wipe the dust from his face, to polish his face with my fingers.

Too overwhelmed to say any of this, I ask about his family instead.

"Your sister? What became of your sister?" I am cautious when I ask this question, knowing that the news might be bad. Indeed it is. I can tell by the way Lokure pulls me to sit on the ground with him. It is easier to discuss bad news down low where your knees won't buckle.

"One of the murahaleen, an Arab militia man on a horse, came and took her." His voice is too many things at once when he speaks. Within it I can hear the sound of mothers keening. "Yes," Lokure says. "This horseman picked her up and disappeared. He had a gun. All I could do was watch him leave."

Lele. I remember her, how she used to follow Lokure everywhere.

"You are not to blame, Lokure."

But I can see he doesn't believe me. I see the shame he carries. I carry it, too.

The night our village was bombed I heard Mama yell, "Run," so I did. I ran as fast as I could without looking back.

Why do I remember so few details about a night when I lost my mother, father, brothers and sister at once? I remember sounds — the sound of bombing, which was so loud that I could not hear out of my left ear for days. I can picture Nakiru, one of our neighbors, bent over her leg with a look of sheer confusion on her face because her leg no longer had a foot attached to it. It was as if someone had played a trick on her, had grabbed her foot and run off with it.

This I remember, yet so many other memories are gone,

as if someone came and snatched them, just like Nakiru's
leg.

Mama used to explain how women endure childbirth.
"When something is so painful, you push this pain away,
then bury it. You bury it in a spot so deep that even you
cannot find it. This is how women are able to bear so many
children, how the impossible becomes possible, something
too big coming through something too small."

Looking into Lokure's eyes, I can tell that he suffers
the opposite problem. He remembers too much. Men do
not know this trick of women, the trick of making things
disappear. Lokure seems to be trapped under memories so
heavy that they push down on his eye sockets. Our men
do not cry, not usually, but Lokure looks as though he is
fighting back tears, the way he keeps gulping hard, as if he
is swallowing stones.

"I saw Lele's face, just before the militia man rode off
with her. She wasn't fighting back. She looked limp, almost
dead," he says.

My mind flashes back to Nadai, to how she desperately
clung to the tree trying to keep from being pulled off it.
Then I picture Lele making her body limp, playing dead
while the militia man carted her off. Maybe this was her
only way of fighting back.

"Where did this horseman take her?"

"That was the last time I saw her before the village was
bombed and we began to walk. After my sister disappeared,
Mama took a rock and pounded it into her own forehead
until blood poured into her eyes. I sat with her all the rest
of that day making sure that, wherever she sat, there were
no stones within her reach.

"When the bombs came, Mama and I walked together for a few days, but then one day she refused to walk anymore. She had terrible stomach cramps, and her hands were shaking. I tried to coax her to keep going. I even told her lions would surely come eat her if she didn't move more quickly, but she kept begging me to let her sit, to keep going without her. My mother said, 'Please, since you were little, I nursed you and gave you everything you wanted. I have never asked you for anything until now, and what I am asking is that you leave me and run on ahead.' When she begged me this way, I felt I couldn't disrespect her wishes. Though it nearly killed me to do so, I left her with a group of women who promised to look after her, and then I ran on ahead. I ran away knowing that I was most likely leaving my mother to her death."

"Lokure, I, too, ran ahead." It is all I can manage to tell him. Our knees are nearly touching as we sit talking. I steal looks at his dark eyes, the lids swollen around them. These are eyes that can no longer close all the way, eyes that have been on guard for too long.

"And your family, Poni? Where are your mother and father?" he asks me.

"I don't know," I tell him. I explain how I have traveled alone, how I have now been assigned a foster mother. "A thorn in my foot, that one. She will beat me if I'm gone too long."

"Let's meet again," he tells me. "Return to this very spot tonight. I have something to give you."

I am mystified. Something to give me? None of us has more than our battered tin cups for food, our bits of corrugated metal for our shelter. Though it is unwise to go and meet any boy alone at night, how can I refuse this boy with the beautiful words who, despite everything I did to him, seems to have forgiven me.

"Maybe I will meet you," I tell him, knowing full well that I wouldn't miss our meeting for anything.

■■■

THAT NIGHT, I TELL my foster mother that I need to collect more firewood. Of course this is a strange lie, since no one goes out past dark for this purpose. However, since the incident when she sat over me and ran her wet fingers across my face, I have learned that nighttime is Loriho's tough time, the time when she talks to the ghost of her lost daughter.

Sure enough, she doesn't even look up when I walk past her.

I make my way cautiously to the place where I first spotted Lokure. You have to be careful at night. When the sun goes down, there is sometimes violence among the different groups — Somalis, Rwandans, Ugandans, Congolese, Turkana — who are now forced to live near one another. Because the askari, the Kenyan police, are so outnumbered, at night they hunker down within their station, refusing to come out even if there are riots outside.

How can peace ever exist when there are so many conflicts even here in Kakuma? Just the other week, a group of Somalis killed two of our boys right inside the camp, strung them up in the tree Jesus-style, the skin of their arms pinned back and stretched like the wings of birds.

The Somalis shouted insults. "Don't bury those boys in

the Muslim section of camp." During all of this the police were sitting in their station with the door locked. No one wanted to take the dead boys down from the trees, thinking it might bring bad luck. Who finally did, I can't say. However, even after the bodies were laid out, we were too scared to hold a funeral service for them, too afraid the Somalis would use this as an excuse to come back and kill more of us.

I spot Lokure sitting so still that I wonder if he is asleep. I make sure I walk in front of him where he can see me. After living in the bush, after learning to keep our ears pricked for wild-animal noises or militia, most of us get startled if approached from behind.

"Lokure," I say, causing him to look up. "You said you wanted to give me something, but I can't begin to imagine what it could be."

Lokure reaches into the waistband of his pants — pants that barely keep themselves up around his skinny hips — and hands me a book.

A book? I stare at it.

"On my way to Kakuma, we walked through a village that had been abandoned, nearly burnt to the ground, but the schoolhouse still stood. I walked through the rubble and found this."

"What book is this?" I still can't believe it.

He looks down and reads its title to me, though it is obvious he knows it by memory. "*Things Fall Apart* by Chinua Achebe. This book changed my life," he tells me. "As I walked across the desert, whenever I had time to stop and rest, I would read this. I read when I was meant to be guarding the rest of our group from lions or hyenas. I read when I was meant to be listening for enemies. Reading helped me calm my fears, to lose myself a bit. I even trained myself to read in the dark."

He puts the book in my hands, then folds my fingers over it as if I will not know what to do with the book otherwise.

"I remember you as being someone who possesses a fine love for learning, Poni," he tells me. "You should read this when you can."

"How do you know this about me?"

"Know what?"

"About my love of learning?"

"I watched so many other girls drop out of school. But you were one of the last ones standing."

What should I feel towards Lokure? The war has taught me to trust no one, and yet here he is offering me a most precious gift, a book that survived the bombings just like us.

"Lokure?" The shrillness of my voice makes him flinch, as though he expects me to hit him as I have in the past. Instead what I say is, "I am glad to see you alive and safe."

He smiles then. His lips are as dry and cracked as the muddy ground, but his smile is easy.

"Do read the book, Poni. You will see why I carried it with me this entire time." He adds, "The last part is torn away, but most of the story is still there."

■ ■ ■

THAT NIGHT, AS I ENTER our shelter, I can see the full moon through the piece of metal we use as a roof, metal that my foster mother says only keeps out every other raindrop during those rare times when it does rain. Certainly the metal does nothing to keep the dust out when the wind blows.

Back home, some of our elders practiced magic. Some could hold their breath under water or bring about the rain. A person can train his body to do all manner of inhuman things — live without food, walk without stopping. Perhaps it should come as no surprise to me that Lokure trained himself to read in darkness.

I squint at the pages. Sure enough, despite the blackness surrounding me, the words eventually pierce through.

Reading Achebe's book, I am transported to a Nigerian tribe, the Igbo, different and yet not so different from my own Didinga people. This story is the first time I have ever known an actual African to write about his experience.

Silently, I acknowledge that I owe much to Lokure for teaching me this new trick of reading in the dark. Stare at the words hard enough, and they eventually take shape. Water from a stone, visible from the invisible.

I don't know what to do with the gratitude I feel towards him. It would be simpler if I didn't owe him anything. Yet as I read, I cannot stop my fond feelings towards Lokure — he who magically pulled a book from the rubble, whose eyes read the same pages I am now reading, whose hands fingered the same pages I am now fingering. But it is also Achebe's book that is making me happy for the first time in so long. Falling into this story allows me to forget my actual life for a while.

For the next few evenings, I spend every free moment I have with the book. Then I reach the book's end, but it is not really the end, only the part where the rest of the book got torn away.

"No," I whisper to myself. Of all the indignities I have suffered, this one is very bad. To be given a taste of something and yet not be allowed to drink one's fill. You would think I would be accustomed to this by now, that I would grow used to being thirsty, but it still hurts. The fact that I cannot find out how the book ends, that I am left stranded, fills me with longing and rage.

I am half tempted to find Lokure and, like the old days, thrash him. "How can you cheat me this way? Do you think it's a funny joke to give me a book with no ending?" I calm myself instead and resolve that some day I will escape from Kakuma. Some day I will find a way out. And, when I do, I will find the rest of the book.

The book is like the rest of my life. Some day I will piece it back together.

—15—

I CANNOT STOP THINKING about Lokure. For so long my body was deprived of food and water, but my mind, too, was deprived of its food. Now my head is swimming with words: Lokure's words and Achebe's words mixing together. I look forward to returning the book because it will give me an excuse to see Lokure again.

The unaccompanied boys have their own sections within the camp. When I reach Block II where Lokure is, I have to scan many faces before finding his. Several boys look up at me when I enter, as though they can sense my female energy. I can see the longing in their eyes. I am the wife they left behind, the mother, the sister. Many of these boys have been without women for so long now.

When I do spot Lokure, something goes limp and sad within me. He is bent over a cooking pot stirring grains. It used to be unusual to see a young man cook, but these boys have become both mother and father to themselves.

I stand and stare for a moment before Lokure notices me.

"Ah, Poni. You have found me doing my woman's work." He seems happy, though, his face shiny with sweat.

"Lokure, you were right. It is an incredible book, one
I won't forget." I give him the book. Then, not knowing
what else to do, I turn and get ready to leave.

"You're not leaving? No, no. Sit down. I want to know
more about what you thought of it."

Lokure's request surprises me. Most of the men I know,
even wise men like my father, usually aren't interested in
hearing a woman's opinion.

"I see why this book changed you," I begin. I fold my
legs under me as I sit across from him. He is gazing at me
expectantly.

Then it is as if something cracks open within me. Suddenly, I find myself spilling all of my thoughts and ideas.

"There was plenty of violence in Okonkwo's village,
and he is often a vicious man, but still, I could understand
his wanting to keep his tribe's traditions alive. The Igbo
people were able to work things out among themselves
before the missionaries arrived. Sometimes they worked
things out in a violent way, but it was the only way they
knew."

"Do you think it was better when the missionaries came
and told the Igbo people that they shouldn't practice such
outdated traditions?" Lokure asks, and I feel as though we
are my father and his friend sitting and discussing issues
together, feel as though we are equals.

"No. I think the missionaries make things worse. They
take over, all the while knowing nothing about the Igbo
culture, not even the language."

"You are clever," Lokure says. "I thought the same
thing." He looks so pleased with me, and I can't help noticing his open smile again. At the same time, a part of me

begins to feel uneasy. I shouldn't let my guard down like this, shouldn't be gazing at Lokure in such a way.

Maybe it is this thought that causes me to speak more sharply. "Still, I'm mad at you for giving me a book with no ending. How can you be content not knowing how the book ends? How is it that you seem to settle for so little all the time?"

"Some book is better than no book, isn't it? Besides, you're smart. Invent your own ending."

"Listen. You may be happy with a partial book. You may be happy with this camp." I realize I am straying from the topic at hand, but I can't stop myself. "Well, not me. I want to get out. I don't know where I'll go, but I'll die if I stay here. Maybe my body won't die, but my brain will. Don't you feel it, too?"

If Lokure is surprised by my outburst, he doesn't show it.

"I miss my old life so much," he says, softly now. "But I have to tell you that finding you has made my life here suddenly bearable." He takes my hand in his. "I thought about you all the time. Even after your cousin beat me, even after you beat me. No one could beat the feelings I have for you out of me."

"You're crazy," I say.

"I think if I can just keep visiting you, if we can keep having these conversations about books and other things, we can save one another, keep one another from going mad."

I want to tell Lokure about the boy I carried on my back. I tried to save him, but I couldn't. I had to put him down. *Don't pin your hopes on me, Lokure. I will disappoint you.*

"I have to return to my foster mother now. I have been gone too long," I tell him.

"You'll visit me again," Lokure says, and this time it seems to be more of a command than a question.

"So that we understand one another, I don't take orders. Not from you, not from anyone."

At this Lokure begins to laugh. "Poni, don't you think I know this already? Believe me when I say that I know you don't like to be bossed around."

"Well, good." Though I am annoyed at Lokure's chuckling, I gather myself up to my full height — not very tall. "Then I might visit you again. If I have time."

This last statement is the biggest joke of all, of course.

All I have is time.

—16—

VISITING WITH LOKURE gives me something to look forward to. He makes up poems and funny rhymes about the sights and sounds inside the camp. I introduce him to the dancing boy, whom he finds as amusing as I do.

Most days I am restless and hollow with hunger. Worry circles me like a swarm of flies. Yet I seem to forget this when I am with Lokure. With him, I feel lighter.

From time to time, charities bring in big bags of donated clothing, and I manage to grab a blue scarf from the disorganized heap. I decide to wear it like a sash. Although my dress is dirty and sweat-stained, the sash covers it with a bit of color. I make sure I wear it when I visit Lokure.

Lokure and I talk as we stroll through the camp together. One day, as we walk, a huge windstorm picks up, stirring everything in its path. Sand pelts our faces. I try to shield my face with my hands, but then I remember my scarf.

Unfurling it, I hold it high, trying to protect Lokure and me from the sand's bite. We sit down. Above us, the scarf looks like blue sky. Dust everywhere, but this blue cloth is as cool as shade.

Lokure and I wait out the storm this way, bathed in blue,

watery shadows. Underneath this blue light, my hair no longer looks yellow. Lokure's skin no longer looks dusty as chalk.

"There is so much I want to know about you, Poni." Lokure has to speak loudly, so as to be heard over the wind.

"Such as?"

"Well, to begin with, what would you do if there was no war, if peace suddenly arrived?"

Peace seems like trying to catch a fish with your bare hands. Still, Lokure is so earnest that I try to answer.

"I would go back to school. I would find books to read, like the one you gave me."

"And I would find a way to write. I have always loved this, as you know."

"You do write beautiful words." I nearly confess to keeping the letter he wrote to me so long ago but hold my tongue.

"But there is something that I want even more," Lokure says.

"Ah, you're greedy. What else could you possibly want?" Lokure looks at me, his gaze so steady that I feel something flap and flutter inside of me. But he does not finish his thought.

"I'll tell you another time," he says softly.

Tell me now, I want to beg. I remember when I took a sip of water and felt my split, tattered tongue come back to life. Sitting with Lokure, here under the shady blue of my scarf, I feel the same way. It is as though something dead is now prickling and tingling its way back to life.

Lokure gently pulls my hand down and, with it, my scarf. Everything goes dusky around us once more.

"The dust storm is done." He motions around us. Somehow the storm ended as quickly as it began.

I wish it hadn't. Wish we were still huddled together within the sand's swirl.

But I don't tell him this. Instead I wrap the scarf around my waist once more.

"Come, Poni. I will walk with you. It will be dark soon, and I want to make sure you get back safely."

But under the scarf was where I felt safe.

■ ■ ■

OUR METAL ROOF has fallen down again. I am standing up on my toes, trying to prop it back up.

"Poni?"

I look up. Is it possible? Do I really see yet another person from my past?

This time it is Tihou, my old classmate. Tihou, whose name means "big head." Tihou, who was one of the top students. Seeing her fills me with wonder and joy.

"I cannot believe I am seeing you. You survived. Tihou, you shrewd girl." We grab hands and squeeze.

"It is a small miracle, yes?"

"You are still the same, still tall," I joke, for she is a long-legged girl, so tall that I have to squint into the sun to see her. "Tell me, did you get placed with a foster family?"

"No. I entered the camp with my older sister. I convinced the guards that my sister is, in fact, my aunt and that she is old enough to take care of me."

"You are a good liar." I pat her on the arm.

"What else do we have these days but our lies?" Tihou's

sentences are slow and careful, as though she has written them out first. "I know we have much news to share, but first I have to tell you something very interesting."

"What's that?"

"Have you heard about the debate club?"

"A debate club here in Kakuma? Really?"

"Yes. A group of people gets together to debate and discuss the issues of the day. Everyone is welcome to join, although it is mostly men there, of course," she says.

"Imagine! You know, I'll say this. Our people are ingenious. Even when there is no food or water, people still find a way to entertain themselves."

"You have to come. There is even a real judge who acts like one of our elders from back home. Your mind is so good and bright, Poni, and you have a quick tongue. You would be good at debating."

I want to tell Tihou that I will go anywhere that she and her beautiful sentences are going, but then I hesitate.

"The problem is my foster mother. She beats me if I am gone too long." I pause. "Then again, if the debate club is at night, it will probably work for me to slip away."

"Good. I can meet you, and we'll go together," Tihou says, and I really can't believe my luck.

Just as Tihou promised, there is a sizable crowd at the debate club. Thabon, a well-respected man who comes from a village near my own, serves as moderator for the evening. He announces the topic. "Do guns hurt us or protect us?" After some deliberation, one group lines up behind the side aiming to prove that guns do hurt people, while another group lines up on the opposite side. I do not see any other women lining up to speak. Still, I have no doubt where my opinion lies, and so I stand within the crowd of men.

"To shoot a gun, anyone can learn how to do this," I tell the crowd. "Even a child of ten or eleven years of age. But guns are not natural. They are cowardly."

Some of the men click their tongues at me, while others hoot.

A man responds, his voice booming. "So you are proposing that we defend ourselves against the North using sweet words? You must fight fire with fire, sister. If they use guns, we use guns. These guns are our only hope for justice."

"Sir, do you think you can shout me down? Well, I can shout, too. You believe guns are a positive thing after you have seen mothers and grandmothers dead on the ground by them? What comes next? We use guns and then the North uses bombs. Should we use bombs, too? When does it end? The boys we ask to carry our guns are our sons and brothers."

I feel alive for the first time in a long while. My tongue, still a patchwork of scar tissue, is working at full force now. I look over at Tihou, and she is smiling. Tihou who, like me, stayed in school.

But then I catch the eye of a man in the crowd. I do not know him, but I see the gesture he makes at me. A slashing motion across his neck.

What is he saying? That he wishes me to be silent? That he wishes to slash my neck, himself?

I do not look away. Instead I meet his gaze and try to burn him with my eyes.

■■■

JUST AS I AM preparing to leave the debate, I see Lokure.
He leaves the crowd of boys he is with and walks towards
me.

"Poni, I heard you speak tonight."

"And? Did you like what I said?" I am waiting for
Lokure to tell me how much he admires my courage, how
much he agrees with the points I made. Instead, he shakes
his head.

"No. While I might agree with what you're saying, it
doesn't do any good to make so many of those men angry.
Can't you see that?"

For a second, I feel like someone has stolen my breath.

Still Lokure continues, "Maybe you shouldn't speak
your mind quite so freely."

I flash back to the man in the crowd, the one who made
the slashing motion towards his neck.

"So what are you telling me? That I should keep quiet?"

"I'm saying that maybe you shouldn't act so much like
a man."

Can this be right? Suddenly, it dawns on me what a fool
I've been. Did I really believe that Lokure regarded me as
an equal? That he cared about my opinions and thoughts?
Lokure may have stood and let me abuse him so long ago,
but I refuse to do the same.

"I understand, Lokure. Well, don't worry. You won't
have to trouble yourself with my opinions any longer. I
move best on my own anyway."

I turn away from him and begin to run. This running is
natural to me, as natural as breathing.

I let Lokure see what was soft inside of me, but it won't happen again. It is safer to be alone, to keep moving.

We have a saying back home: "Grass the cattle graze on produces no weeds."

—17—

BACK IN CHUKUDUM, the seasons were what held meaning. In Kakuma, however, the short rains mean little. Our whole way of life is gone. Would it be harvest time back home? What of all the cattle we left behind? For us, cattle were our way of life.

I remember the cool days heavy with mist back in Chukudum. I remember the blankets of blue flowers that used to blossom after the rains.

Everyone here in the camp has lost loved ones, but speaking of these huge losses is too much. Instead, people speak of the smaller ones — that special pot for grinding grains, the beads they used to put on for special occasions. "I wonder where those ended up," people murmur.

Because thinking of my family brings too much hurt, I think of other people from my past. What became of my teacher with his large black-rimmed glasses, for example? But thinking of him also brings pain, because it reminds me that every month that passes is another month during which I am no longer attending school. Now I avoid going to the debate club for fear of seeing Lokure. My mind is starving once again.

I must leave Kakuma. The problem is, I have no idea where to go. Because I know how to brew beer, I can earn a small amount of money by selling it to those Kenyans working in the camp. The Kenyan guards, aid workers and teachers still have some shillings. I know I need money if I am to leave, so I try to focus my energy on this task.

The only other small joy that I have is dancing. It is what we women do to remind ourselves that we are still alive, to remind ourselves of the joys we once knew. Even those of us who are starving, who are weak, when we hear a certain drumbeat, something stirs in us. Suddenly, even the elderly come alive, turn young, hop up and down, stomp their feet and clap. I push off the ground and send myself up into the air before allowing the ground to pull me back down. I don't want to stop. When I dance, I can jump out of my pain for just a moment. I can get that much closer to God, to yell straight into his ear.

Have you forgotten that we are still here?

■ ■ ■

ON ONE OF MY BAD mornings when I am sitting outside my shelter running my hands over all the places where my ribs pucker against my skin, Tihou comes to me yet again.

"Ah, Tihou. You are the only one who can bring me good cheer. Have you come to make time?"

"Actually, I'm here on a mission. First, a question. Are you hungry?"

"Is this is a trick question? Show me someone here who isn't hungry. In fact, just before you came, I was thinking my bones might poke through my skin."

"Okay, then. So, how many names were given to you at your naming ceremony?" Tihou asks me.

I list my full name for her. "Zenitra Lujana Paul Poni."

"Good. I have learned something we can do to get more food. You just have to trust me and be willing to break a few rules."

I do trust Tihou, and I have always loved breaking rules, so naturally I follow her. "We actually have to leave the camp temporarily," Tihou explains. "Just do as I do."

I nod. We walk all the way to the west edge of the refugee camp, near the barbed-wire fences. We reach a spot where people can enter the camp. Instead, we start to make our way out.

One of the guards spots us leaving and shouts, "Hey!"

Tihou casts her eyes down, then hands something to the guard. "For you." It is kitu kidogo, bribe money. I don't know how she has managed to come by it.

"Do you plan on returning?" the guard demands. I see Tihou eyeing his gun. Her body seems to tilt. She looks as though she may fall down.

It is then that I take over, walk right to the guard.

"We'll return," I tell him. "But you'll let us pass now, yes?" He looks at the shillings in his hands and then signals that we may go through.

"You are braver than me, Poni," Tihou says. "I was so nervous, I couldn't breathe."

"Are you going to tell me what we're doing now?"

"We have to walk around to the opposite entrance of the camp. When we get there, we pretend that we are new arrivals. This is the clever part. We will receive an entirely new food ration card."

"Do you think it will work?"

"I was told it would," Tihou says, and so we try out her plan. We walk all the way to the other check-in point several miles away. When the security guard asks us our names, I quickly choose one of my other ones — Zenitra. Lucky for me I have so many names to spare.

Unbelievably, the guard accepts my statement as fact and gives me a new identification and ration card. Suddenly, I am not one person, but two.

When Tihou and I are out of earshot of the guard, we examine our new cards.

"More food for each of us," Tihou says. "Once we reach the front of the queue, we will simply circle back and return a second time."

"What if the guard in the food line recognizes us?" I ask.

"Apparently they don't do anything to stop you. Besides, are you not both Poni and Zenitra?" She slaps me playfully on the arm.

"Oh, yes. I am all these people at once." I laugh. Oh, when is the last time I have laughed like this? Tihou laughs, too — laughs until I can see the full length of her throat.

It is a welcome change to focus on Tihou's outstretched throat and her surprisingly deep laugh instead of having to look into her eyes, cloudy with dust and loss. Some individuals carry their grief in their shoulders, others in the jutted-out parts of their jaw or lips. Tihou keeps her grief in her chest. The weight of it causes her to lean forward slightly when she walks.

When Tihou catches me watching her, it is as though she knows what I am thinking.

"I lost everyone but my sister, Poni. Do you remember my father?"

"He was a very honored man."

"Well, my father was very active in the church. Because of this, the Northerners targeted him. Oh, and they did not just kill him quickly," Tihou tells me. "They did like this and this." She makes a cutting motion. "Cut, cut, cut. His ears they did one by one. Then they cut the tip of his nose. I couldn't watch the rest. After this, my sister and I ran and hid. When we returned, he was lying there dead, all parts of him gone, even his fingers. My mother was dead next to him, though her they did not cut."

I can feel my mouth open in horror. "Maybe this is what happened to my father, too."

"No," Tihou says. "Nothing like that. I am sure of it."

I look at her, so grateful for her lie.

—*18*—

EVERY DAY IS THE SAME in the camps. Find out who has died. Line up for food rations. We cannot provide for ourselves, cannot raise our crops or our cattle here. All we can do is wait with our hands out.

One morning I get up very early and, carrying both of my ration cards, get in the food line. I am grateful for my two cards, for we have been without food all week, but this also means that I will be in line all day, first as one of my selves and then as another. And then there is the small part of me that knows that taking an extra ration means that someone else may miss theirs. Still, the promise of food banishes all other thoughts from my head.

Each day that I wait in line, someone drops dead from the heat, from the fatigue, from the futility. Some people make it to the front only to find that all the food is gone.

This is how it goes.

On this particular day, as I stand in the food line, I notice the way the sky pinks as the sun comes up. The pink-and-gold beauty of this sunrise is a mockery in the face of so much ugliness, like a woman wearing her printed dress while, around her, everyone else stands naked. My legs ache already, and yet I have so many hours of waiting and standing ahead of me.

As the morning sun comes to life, she releases her scorch and fury upon those of us waiting in line. The heat has a rhythm to it. It taps me on my exposed arms and legs. It throbs inside my temples. I sway my arms from side to side as if I can magically create a breeze, but, no. The heat presses itself into me like a second skin.

Some people leave the queue and then return. When they do, they mark their place in line with a particular jerry can or sometimes a stone. They must return quickly, though, or their marker will be moved. Some of the people in line lean on tall sticks. Others squat low because they are too old or too weak.

Suddenly, there is a stirring within the line. A woman, all ribs except for a pregnant belly, is muttering.

"If it was just me, but I am with baby. I need food for the baby." She begins to weave her way forward, trying to move up in the line. "Baby, baby," she says. The others standing in line gently bump her away, put out elbows or a knee to keep her from cutting into their section. The woman looks dazed, as if she does not know where she is. I motion to her to come stand in line with me. But as I am doing so, some security guards, whose job it is to walk up and down and monitor the food line, catch sight of her. One of them says something to her that makes her clasp her hands together in desperation.

The next thing I know, the security guards are beating her with a club. They do not hit her hard. It is more like they are swatting at an annoying mosquito or fly. After one or two taps with their club, she topples over and lands on her side, making a flesh-hitting-dirt sound.

One of the Kenyan guards carries her off, telling whoever is within earshot that he is going to get her some medical attention, but I do not believe this. I am fairly certain that both the woman and the baby are dead. If not now, then soon.

—19—

IT IS NOT THAT THERE are no doctors here, but there are so few of them to go around. Two trained doctors for 85,000 refugees and a handful of nurses, mostly untrained. Not more than a week after the guards hit the pregnant woman from the food line, a different pregnant woman, one who sleeps near me, starts vomiting loudly enough to wake me. When I go to her, her whole body jolts on the ground as if electricity is traveling through it. Her eyes show only their whites.

"Hey, hold steady," I yell. There is a doctor from Médecins sans Frontières who works in our part of the camp, but he does not start working again until the morning, and here it is still the middle of the night. I have nowhere to take this jolting woman.

I throw myself on top of her, sit astride her round stomach. I try to hold her mouth open so that she can breathe. Her thrashings are so violent that I am afraid she will throw me off, and yet I continue to ride her.

Finally, her body stills, but her head rolls from side to side. Her eyes fix on me, but they do not see.

"Wait until morning," I tell her. "The doctor will come.

You will be saved then, but you must wait and hold on."
She seems to hear me, because her eyes move upwards, towards the sky. I see her eyes searching, searching.

Are they looking for the first ray of light? For God? Her
eyes stay like this, peering upwards, looking round and
round.

She does not last until morning, dies with her hand lying
atop her bulging belly. As the sun rises, two men carry her
off in their bare arms.

As if seeing another pregnant woman die isn't enough,
on this day my foster mother tells me, "I will be marrying you off soon. There are several men in our camp who
have already offered me a decent bride price for you. Now
I must simply choose."

"What men?" I want to ask, but it doesn't matter what
men. I would sooner die than be married off.

I must leave Kakuma right away. But where to go?

Suddenly an idea comes into my head. It is so crazy that
I almost laugh aloud. People have told me about the United Nations building that is within walking distance of the
main entrance at the other side of the camp. The people
who work there are said to be peacekeepers. Maybe they
need to know how bad things are in the camp. Perhaps
someone in this building will listen to me.

I know this much. The building is for officials, not displaced people. Still, I cannot help thinking that, if I make
my way inside the building, I might find someone who can
help me leave Kakuma.

I rise early, before my foster mother has woken up. At
the west entrance of the camp, I do what Tihou taught me
and use my home-brew money to bribe the guards to let me

leave and then return. Then I start walking the long way around the camp towards the UN compound as though this is the most natural thing to do.

People pass me on the road. "Where are you going, eh?" they ask.

"I am going to the UN building."

They shake their heads. "You cannot just go there." But I ignore them. Let the UN guards turn me away. I will be no worse off.

Someone mutters, "That building is protected by guards with guns. They will fire at you."

Maybe my fatigue has made me bold. Maybe my foolishness will march me straight into death's mouth. Maybe I no longer care. I keep walking.

As I walk, I pass a group of Turkana women along the side of the road. Their necks are held straight and tall by huge beaded necklaces, but everything else on them sags into the dirt as they crawl about, trying to find bits of coal to sell.

I only have to walk an hour to reach the UN compound. The building is surrounded by a tall, jagged barbed-wire fence. The door to the building looks heavy and official. A Kenyan guard stands out front and does, in fact, hold a terrifying rifle at his side. A feeling of panic rises in me.

Still, I force myself to approach this man.

"What do you need?" he asks me.

Tihou taught me how to lie, how to be more than one person if I have to. Today I will be someone new, someone who has a reason to go inside that building.

"I have a meeting with someone who works here. Manute is inside waiting for me." Manute is a common name, and I am just praying someone with this same name actually works there.

The man consults a typed list on a clipboard. "Manute Deng? That one?"

"Him. Yes."

"He didn't leave word with me."

"He must have forgotten. We made this meeting weeks ago, and I have come a long way to get here."

I can see this guard sizing me up. He is most likely puzzling over my dirty appearance, but the thought must also cross his mind that no one would be stupid enough — would risk getting shot — to come to the UN building without reason.

"He is expecting you?"

"Yes. I am actually a bit late to meet him," I reply. The guard pats me down to make sure I am not carrying weapons, as though I could conceal anything inside my thin dress.

"You may go in, and I will phone Manute Deng to let him know you're on your way."

I nod. This man will be quite confused by this phone call, but at least I will get inside the building.

The UN building is like an entire city inside. The first thing I feel is actual air-conditioning. I have heard of this fake air, but have never experienced it before. The cold air seems to come from all directions, making me shiver. The floors are not made of dirt but are shiny and solid. I am scared because I do not know where to go inside this compound, but I start walking. Walk as if you are going somewhere, and maybe no one will question you.

A white woman approaches me, and I feel my heart

pound. White skin used to make me nervous when I was very young, until I got to know a few of the missionaries who passed through our village. This woman smiles and asks if she can help me. She speaks a strange mix of English and Kiswahili, which I am somehow able to follow.

Her hair is long and yellowy, but her outfit of trousers and a blouse is as gray as stone. Her black shoes make a clicking noise on the hard floor, unlike my own bare feet.

At any moment, guards may find me and throw me out, and so I begin to talk, to tell this woman everything. About how I have only recently seen two pregnant women die before my eyes, about how my foster mother is arranging a marriage for me, about how I want to go to school.

The woman says, "I see..." several times as I talk. She does not try to stop me until I am finished speaking. Instead she says, "I know how bad it is in the camps. Appalling, really. That's why I came to work here. To try to help." Then she adds, "Let me take you to lunch. You can tell me more."

Suddenly, her white hand is on my arm, and she is leading me down the hallway. Perhaps she will have me arrested, yet I have nothing to do but walk with her. As we go, the woman points out the various rooms of the building.

"This is the squash court. This is the swimming pool." She speaks to me in a breezy way, as if I am an official visitor and not a half-dead refugee from the camp. She does not seem to think that having a big swimming pool here inside the building, here within the middle of the desert, is unusual.

After living in a dust bowl, after watching people fall down and die of dehydration, to see this enormous pool full of clean, clear water is too much.

Oh, that I could jump into the swimming pool, surround myself with water, drink it. Yet the workers in this building use this pool for playing and floating? How did they manage to transport all of this water into the swimming pool? Did they drive past all of the dying refugees in the camps with their water tanks?

And what to think of this UN woman? She is kind enough to listen to me, has not had me arrested as of yet. I want to prostrate myself to her and, at the same time, claw her eyes out.

Is this fair for you to be living like this — cold air coming at you from all sides — while right outside people are being cooked alive? What if the pregnant woman had found her way here? Would she be alive now?

Being in the UN is like visiting another world, and yet it is so very close to the camp, so close you can walk right to it.

"Are you okay?" she asks me.

"Yes. Thank you." I learned from my mother how to bend my head and hide the emotions of my face.

"At least we can get one good meal into you. Not that this cafeteria food is so good, mind you," she laughs. "All of us who work here joke about how bad the food is." I try to laugh, but the horror of it is almost too much to bear.

As though she can read my thoughts, the woman is suddenly talking again. "I want to help. Really I do. I mean, I joined the UN to help people, to help Africa. I thought about going to Mozambique. They had a position open there, and there are beautiful beaches, but when I heard about this whole mess in Sudan, I said, no, let me go there, where I can really be of some use. But you know how it is.

I mean, there are so many people who are dying all the time that you just feel too helpless in the face of it all. How do you stop all of these killings? All of this starvation?"

I know I lied to get into this building, that this woman is allowing me to stay by her good graces alone, but what does she want me to say? That she is fighting for a noble cause? Cleaning up our mess for us? That she is one of the few Westerners who bothers to care? Yes, I know she is a good person and means well. Yet, dear lady, how can you really see what is going on outside from in here? From this building with its swimming pool and fake air?

"Do you ever go inside the camp?" I ask. I am hoping that it is a general enough question not to cause offense.

"I do, although the UN is very concerned for our safety and limits our mobility. None of the aid organizations are allowed to stay in the camp past five in the evening because of all of the violence. It's horrible there. All the suffering. Everyone wanting me to save them. People think I'm a doctor, that I might have medicine, but I don't. I'm here as an administrator. Back home in the US people have barely even heard of your civil war."

The way she says this sounds odd to my ears. It sounds as though she thinks the war belongs to me personally.

"We send reports back, but officials there are squabbling over whether or not to classify this situation as genocide. They should just help, rather than worrying about numbers." Then she changes the topic. "You wanted lunch, right?"

As we enter the cafeteria, my mind can barely take in the sight of all the food. There is fruit arranged in pyramids, as if the food itself is a decoration. There are slices of meat cut thinly and rolled up as if they are on display, and there is an enormous pot of hot beef stew with huge chunks of vegetables.

As if this is not enough, there are actual bins that dispense cereal, cold sodas and bottles of water.

How many people could this food save? I can feel the saliva fill my mouth, and I imagine sticking my face straight into the bowl of stew, slurping it up like a cow. Yet I remember hearing how people can become deathly ill from eating too much after having nothing for so long. I know I must be careful, that my stomach is now a shrunken fruit pit.

The UN woman urges me on. "You should eat what you can. I know they barely give you anything inside the camp."

I point to a coffee cup. "This is how much grains we get. Sometimes it has to last a week." I try to eat with some grace, but I am aware that I am shoving rolls of meat into my mouth before I have time to chew.

The woman does not seem to notice.

"Poni," she finally says. I realize I must have told her my name in the beginning, and she has remembered it, even though I never asked for hers. "I appreciate having the opportunity to talk with you." The way she talks, she makes it sound as though I have somehow done her a favor. She doesn't know or care that I lied my way into this building, that some man named Manute is most likely searching the halls for me.

"Usually I'm not allowed to help individual people," the UN woman says. "I'm not very high up here. Plus, you know how it is. Help one person, and suddenly you have a line of a hundred standing with their hands out. But I like you. I can tell you're really smart."

How does she know this about me?

"Have you ever heard of Sister Hannah?" she continues.

I shake my head.

"She's a nun who lives just outside Nairobi. She is known to help girls. Tell me, where do you live inside the camp?"

"Section 10D." I can't help it. I am still licking the meat juice off my fingers.

"I can come get you and take you to the nun. As I said, I'm not really supposed to help people from the camps, but I want to help you. The thing is, others might want to come along, so you'd have to keep this a secret."

Who would I tell? I do not even know this UN woman's name.

"And the pregnant women who died in the camp?" I say.

"Well, they're already dead..." The woman lets her voice trail off. "We can't really help them now. Better to focus on the living, no?"

The woman has missed the point, but then, I do not know exactly what my point is, either. What did I expect her to do? Bring dead women back to life?

"Anyway, I'll come for you within the next few days," the woman says. "Can you be ready?"

"Yes." I have nothing to pack. I own nothing. I have been ready to go for some time now. "I cannot thank you enough."

"Let me walk you out of the building. That way the guard won't give you any problems," she says. Seeing me eye the bowl of fruit on one of the tables, she grabs several oranges. "Tuck these into the fold of your skirt and take them with you." I nod and follow her, keeping my head ducked down. Somehow I have managed to elude Manute Deng. Now I just need to make it to the exit.

It is hard making my way out of the UN building, saying goodbye to the air-conditioning, the dust-free air, the people who walk through the halls looking as though they have important business. I wish I could drag the pot of beef stew out with me, to fill my skirt with bottles of water, but I know I cannot.

"I will wait for you," I call out. The woman nods before disappearing back into the building, the building that already seems like a dream to me.

Now I am back outside with the heat and the flies. I walk back to camp, back to my foster mother who is surely waiting for me with her acacia branch.

■ ■ ■

AS PREDICTED, MY foster mother does beat me upon my return. She calls me a prostitute and accuses me of sneaking off to couple with a man. I want to laugh in spite of the pain her thrashing is causing me. This is where she thinks I have been?

The truth is, though, I do find myself thinking about Lokure. There is a foolish part of me that wants to tell him goodbye before the UN woman comes for me, but as soon as I think this, I remind myself of how our last meeting ended. Best not to see him ever again.

Yet the next day, as I am going to fetch firewood, there he is. I pretend not to notice him, but he comes right to me.

"Hey, Poni."

"I'm busy," I tell him sharply.

"Why did you run away from me when we last spoke? Why are you avoiding me?"

"You really don't know? You're the one who told me that I should stay silent, that I should control myself."

Lokure laughs, and I really do feel like beating him.

"Poni, do you ever give people a chance to explain themselves?"

"Explain, then," I say, anger still coursing through me.

"Believe me, I know that I can't silence you, nor would I want to, but seeing how you incited those men made me afraid for you. I want to protect you."

"I don't need protecting. You should have realized that by now."

Lokure stops chuckling. How his face can shift, from amused to solemn, in just a moment's time.

"Have I not made it clear all that I feel for you? I have been trying to win your love for so long now. I have never stopped thinking you were beautiful or admiring your boldness, but I don't want to lose you."

A long moment passes. I cannot think of what to say.

Lokure continues, "I have lost too many people to violence already. I don't wish to stand by while something bad happens to you, too."

"I can care for myself. I have survived so far." But I can hear my resolve weakening.

"I know you're fearless. It's me who is afraid." Lokure pauses to wipe sweat away from the sides of his face. "I told you what happened to my mother, but I never told you about my father. A few days after my sister disappeared, some SPLA soldiers came to question him. They were looking for more boys to join the army and had a list with my name on it. 'Where is your son?' they asked him. He answered that I was visiting an aunt in a nearby village. It was the truth. After my sister's kidnapping, my mother and I went there thinking we would be safer. Still, the soldiers assumed I was a deserter. They shot my father, left him there in the dust. My neighbor saw the whole thing happen."

A single tear trickles down, mixing with the dirt on Lokure's face, as if he is crying mud.

I stand there, unable to respond. I want to take some of Lokure's pain from him, to lessen his load, but this cannot be done. We all must carry our pain. Carry it until it gets so heavy that we have no choice but to lay it down.

"I see you speaking out in front of a group of men at debate club, and I'm scared for you. Will the men come for you? I have lost everyone that I love, but not you."

Hearing Lokure's words, I want to reach out to him. Yet, I am still doubtful. Lokure wants to protect me, but he also wants to silence me.

"Lokure, your problem with me is not only that I speak too loudly. Perhaps I am not gentle enough for you."

Lokure's voice is thick now. "You should know I still think all parts of you beautiful, even your wild tongue." As if sensing I am about to protest, he adds, "And I will never be the person telling you not to go to school. I believe what our teacher used to tell us. Do you remember? He said that education is the only hope for peace. This war will end, Poni. I have to believe that. I just want you safe until then. That is all I am asking. God is constantly testing me. I don't want to be tested anymore. I am so tired." He looks right into my eyes. "Lele never had a chance to survive. You do."

I am surprised by the sound that emerges from my mouth — half human, half animal — and then my head is on Lokure's chest, and he is holding the back of my head with one hand, the other arm dangling loose at his side. I can feel myself surrendering to him, tucking myself into the hollow of his chest.

Within this one moment of our bodies touching, I immediately know everything about him. Neither of us has the luxury of excess flesh to hide our secrets. We have been whittled down, the two of us, and now I can feel every part of Lokure — his bones, his organs, his heart — that internal drum longing to be set free. I know he can feel every dried-out, sharp-angled part of me as well. Lokure is like a tree offering me momentary shade.

How can I refuse this comfort, this human contact? Truly, it has been so long. But at the same moment that I am thinking this, I am also reminding myself that I have to leave. I promised the UN woman I would come alone.

Yet how to leave Lokure behind?

Though it makes my throat ache with pain, I pull myself out of Lokure's arms.

"I have an opportunity to leave, to go to a nun in Nairobi who takes in girls." I see the look that passes across his face, a look of sad resignation. He will lose me, too.

Part of me hopes that he will beg me to stay. But he doesn't. Instead he forces a smile onto his face.

"I told you all I wanted was for you to be safe. If you have an opportunity to leave, you have to take it. Leave, and don't look back."

"What about you?"

"I'll find a way to escape. I'm strong, too."

Legs like sticks, and yet it's true. He brushes his fingers along the side of my cheek. Fingers that are callused but soft like grass.

"I'm happy knowing you'll be safe. I'll find a way to be with you again." He should know how dangerous it is to make a promise like this.

"Your words, Lokure, I know it is selfish of me, but I need more of your words to keep me going." And then I tell him everything. I tell him about the letter I never destroyed, the words that I memorized.

Lokure laughs, as if this is the funniest thing he has heard. "Ah, the truth comes out. I knew you couldn't resist my charms."

"Now you know," I tell him. "Your words helped me more than you could have imagined, but I've used them up now. I need more of them to take with me. Please, Lokure. Don't make me beg."

"I have so many more words to give you. I've been saving them all this time." Then he bends and whispers words into my ear, words that cause the skin on my neck to prickle under his hot breath, words that make the flies around us momentarily fade away. I devour these words, but I also try to ration them, to shove them into the folds of my skirt.

What if this is all I will ever be able to keep of him? What if this is all I can take with me?

"I wish I had something to give you in return."

"You have already given me what I crave. You were the thing I wanted. I was waiting to tell you."

"I won't forget you." So many of my memories are now

in a deep place that I can't reach, but I won't forget this one. I take Lokure's hand, and we stand like this. For once, I don't want time to move.

I can't look back at him when I finally turn to leave. The pain that radiates through me nearly stops me from walking away.

But I do. My legs never forget how.

■ ■ ■

I TRY TO AVOID MY foster mother, but when I do see her, she tells me, "I have found a man who sells tobacco here in the camp. A good businessman. He has earned enough money to offer a bride price. He has other wives, but who knows if they survived or not?"

Am I to be a replacement wife? First a replacement daughter and now a replacement wife? Oh, how little my foster mother knows. I almost laugh angrily in her face. You will try to marry me off? Ha! But I will be long gone.

The UN woman is coming to save me any day, any hour.

I want this to be true. My eyes are always craning, waiting to spot the UN woman wandering through the camps. I look everywhere for pale skin and yellowy hair. My legs jiggle and itch with readiness. At night I hardly sleep. I promised the UN woman I would be ready to leave. And who knows? Perhaps she will fetch me during the night.

I picture the UN woman appearing and softly motioning for me to follow her. The two of us would glide out of camp together. She would usher me into an air-conditioned car and take me to the nun. I would thank her profusely, of course, shake her hand or maybe embrace her, if this is what white people prefer.

I watch and wait for her. I do this for a whole week.

Finally, I accept the truth.

She isn't coming.

She said it herself. "Help one person and you have to help so many more."

Did I really think that I was important enough for her to save? No. There is no use relying on others.

If I am going to escape, I must do it on my own. Now that I know about Sister Hannah, I must go to her myself. It is my only chance.

Tihou is the only one with whom I share my plan. As expected, she is full of ideas. Thanks to my beer sales, I already have enough money for a lorry ticket. Tihou, meanwhile, has a small map of Kenya that she helps me study.

"You must come with me, Tihou." Though I can't bring Lokure with me, bringing another female, another girl at risk, should not hurt my chances with Sister Hannah.

"I need to stay and take care of my sister. She is not well enough to travel." Tihou's sister has tuberculosis. It is obvious from her coughing and fever.

"What if you left your sister behind?" I wait to see how Tihou will react to my harsh suggestion.

"You think my sister is going to die?"

I should lie, just as Tihou did when she assured me that my father wasn't tortured. Yet I also feel an absolute desperation to get Tihou out of the camp, both for her sake and my own. We will be so much safer traveling together.

I know I am asking Tihou to turn her back on her sister. I am asking her to be as cruel as I am.

But I cannot stop myself. "I know you are doing the right thing, Tihou, helping your sister, but perhaps you can find others who could care for her. As for you, this might be your only chance to escape. They say Sister Hannah is able to save the girls who find their way to her."

If Tihou is angry with me, she does not show it. "You're right to tell me all this. I don't like hearing it, but you're right."

"Come with me, Tihou. After the war, we'll pray to God for forgiveness. We'll pray that we made the right choice trying to save ourselves. But we have to escape. We have to find a way to go to school again."

"I'm all my sister has left," Tihou replies. I can see her deliberating. A decision like this can instantly turn you old. I see Tihou's shoulders turn inward, see her spine sag.

"My sister needs me," she finally says. "She may still get better. There is a Red Cross volunteer, and if we just wait, we might be able to get help."

Ah, yes, the Red Cross line. Person after person waiting in the heat in order to see one overworked doctor. Yet this is Tihou's decision.

I think back to my own mother. She told me to run, and I did. But if I had known I wouldn't see her again, would I still have made the same choice?

"I accept your decision, yet it's so painful leaving you."

"I will get by," Tihou says, and I try to believe her.

■ ■ ■

OVER THE NEXT WEEK, I busy myself with preparations. Tihou learns from one of the other women how to obtain a lorry ticket from Kakuma to Lodwar. From there I can take a minivan to Kitale and, finally, a bus to Nairobi.

The day before I am to leave, I visit Tihou one last time.

"You've got to be wary of the Somali shifta," Tihou tells me. "I heard someone say that bandits look to steal and even kill people." Then she adds, "I know you'll make it, Poni. You'll find your way to the nun." I take Tihou's hand and hold it. "I want you to have these." Tihou gives me a pair of simple gold-colored hoop earrings. "It is good to have something to sell if you need to."

"I can't take these from you."

"You have to. They'll bring you good fortune," she insists.

A long time ago I had holes in my ears. But, like the rest of me, these holes are now covered over with scar tissue. Still, I take these earrings and force them in, feel the skin pop as I push them through the lobes.

"These will always remind me of you, Tihou," I tell her. Then, as if I am channeling the voice of Mama, I say, "Promise me that you will continue your schooling, Tihou. Find a way."

"You know I'll try."

Before leaving, I enter Tihou's shelter to look upon her sister. Agii is even more ill than when I last saw her. Her eyes are now unfocused. Her teeth are starting to bare. It is a look I know too well now. Death has already begun to claim bits of her. It is only a matter of days or weeks before it claims her entirely. Tihou cradles her sister in her arms and tries to give her a small bit of water.

"Ask God to pray for us, Poni," Tihou says quietly, a look of absolute grief upon her face.

I could wait for Agii to die. Tihou could come with me.

But then I think of my foster mother and the man she has chosen for me to marry, a man who sells tobacco and has many wives.

No, I know I cannot stay, not one day more.

—20—

WHAT MAKES YOU THINK *you can leave? Thousands re-main in Kakuma, and yet you have the nerve to escape.* The voice in my head sounds like that of my foster mother, all its soft edges worn away by fatigue and disappointment.

But then I hear my mother's voice, and it drowns out this first one. *Do not listen to this, Chi Chi. Just leave quietly and then, as soon as you can, run. Run like you always do.*

I walk out of the shelter on the balls of my feet, do not even look at my foster mother. As soon as I reach the fence, I give the guards their bribe, and then, as soon as I am past the camp's exit, I run without looking back. I leave it all behind: the cracked ground that resembles old skin, the slabs of tin that try to pass for roofs, the women who stand with their backs bent over the small amounts of grain they are trying to turn into a meal.

Though I know my foster mother is counting on the bride money I will bring her, I do not pity her. With or without me, she will continue to talk to the ghost of her dead daughter, will hang somewhere between life and death.

Yet, leaving Lokure behind is too painful. I borrowed so

132

much from him — first his book and then his words — but left him with nothing. Maybe I am selfish. Maybe my heart is harder than most people's.

Those fingers of yours, Lokure, like tall grass — gentle and rough at the same time.

I believe I will miss your fingers as much as I will miss your words.

—21—

I AM SITTING ON A BUS, and as I look out the pock-
marked window, I see the brown barrenness recede behind
me. I am finally emerging from a dust storm, rubbing my
eyes to clear them.

The color green. Ah! How long has it been since I have
seen this color? Back in dry Kakuma, this color was absent,
as though someone had spirited it away, but now it is everywhere.

I touch the earrings Tihou gave me. These are all that I
own. I no longer even have undergarments, having washed
the only pair I owned so many times that they eventually
fell apart in my hands. There is little left to cover me other than my worn-thin dress. Luckily, I have not had my
monthly bleedings for some time now, probably because of
how thin I am.

The bus heaves and shakes as we ride from Kitale
through Eldoret and Nakuru. I remember when I rode on
top of the pregnant woman having a seizure. The bus is no
different. It seems to want to throw me off.

I look out the window and see sights that stir my soul.
Pink flamingos lining the edges of Lake Nakuru, zebras

near Naivasha, an occasional giraffe off in the distance. And colors of all kinds. Such colors.

Here, too, is yet another bit of strangeness. My body is cold for the first time in so long. In Kakuma the air was hot enough to scorch me like a cooking stove. Yet now I am shivering. A clingy gray mist surrounds the bus, strange but also familiar. I know this mist, of course. It is the same mist we had in the Didinga Hills, the mist of my childhood.

I try to let this thought calm my worries. The fact is, paying for the bus used up the last shilling I own. If Sister Hannah does not take me in, I will have absolutely no place to go.

■ ■ ■

WE REACH NAIROBI and alight from the bus. Unlike Kakuma, with its tired land and people, Nairobi is a busy, bustling town: Kikuyu women wearing hip length sweaters, Maasai women dressed in red shukas, vendors selling hair-braiding, firewood, blankets and vegetables. As I walk, a white taxi narrowly dodges around me, and I find myself laughing crazily.

After all that I have survived, all the near-misses, to be hit by a careless taxi? That would be a way to die? I must be more careful, and yet I am dizzy with all these new sights and sounds. The scents are almost too much — a blend of human excrement, burning rubbish, and also the sweet perfume of the purple jacaranda tree.

Suddenly, a street boy charges at me. I don't see his face. All I see are his hands flying out in front of me. There is a burning, like fire, in both of my earlobes. I clap my hands to my ears and howl.

It does not take me long to discover that this thief has ripped Tihou's earrings right out from my ears. The earrings are gone, and both my earlobes are now torn into two pieces.

Why was I so vain as to wear my only jewelry? Why did I forget the cautions I heard about the street boys in Nairobi?

"Mwizi! Thief!" I scream as loudly as I can and point in the direction of the young street boy. A few men give chase to him, and so do I, but soon it is apparent that this one is a good runner and has disappeared.

Will my earlobes mend as my tongue did or remain torn apart forever? I pinch my ears as hard as I can, try to squeeze the pain away. It doesn't work. These earlobes of mine will throb for days, both from discomfort and indignity.

■■■

FINALLY, AFTER WALKING all day, I reach Sister Hannah's compound. There are several simple white cement buildings. The one in front is guarded by armed police.

I have heard this place is safe, that Sister Hannah is able to protect those she shelters. But of course I was told this about Kakuma as well.

I take a deep breath and start to walk towards the guard. However, just as I draw near, I hear a female voice speaking harshly.

"Shoo, shoo. Go on and shoo." I look to see who is yelling in such a manner.

To my surprise, it is Sister Hannah. At least I assume it is her, since she is wearing a nun's habit and has white skin. This woman she is yelling at is an older Sudanese woman with shorn hair and rheumy eyes.

"Please. Take pity, take pity." The cloudy-eyed woman clasps her hands together.

"No, no. We are full up here. Go elsewhere," Sister Hannah yells. "Go back to the camps. I am sorry, but you must get your help there."

"There is nothing for me there."

"I am terribly sorry, but I can't help you at this time."

Before Sister Hannah can turn to see me, I run and hide in an empty duka, a small stand where people go to purchase matches, batteries or fried samosas.

Imagine getting chased away by a nun. And I might be next. I watch through a muddy window as Sister Hannah turns and heads back into the compound. The woman who was begging turns and walks away, too.

I feel my hope drain. Have I come all this way only to learn that Sister Hannah is not accepting new girls? This nun is nothing like I expected. Her temper seems as fiery as my own, and this is not a good thing.

I stay in the duka for nearly an hour, trying to think what to do, trying to calm my nerves. As I am crouching there, one of the shamba boys, a gardener, comes near. He is holding a pair of clippers. He walks towards the bushes, but then he turns towards my hiding place.

"Tsk, tsk, you. What are you hiding from?" he asks.

"I was told to come here and find Sister Hannah, but now I am worried she'll turn me away."

This tufty-haired boy laughs at me.

"Why is this humorous, brother?" I ask.

"I am not laughing to be mean," he says. "But around here, everyone knows you must approach Sister when she is in good spirits, not bad."

"And when will this be, that I will find her in good spirits?"

Again he laughs. "You think I know? You think I can predict the future?"

"Will you let me stay here for now? This is my only hiding place for the time being."

"Well, all right. There are many bushes I need to trim, but I will return soon, so don't stay here too long. Good luck to you, sistah..." His voice trails off as he walks away, his big clippers hanging from one hand.

God is weary of my prayers. Perhaps this is why I pray to Lokure instead. Lokure, lend me some really choice words to win the good graces of Sister Hannah. This is my only option, to talk my way into her favor. What else is there for me to do?

I walk slowly towards the guards. When one spots me, I hand him the lie that has become as worn through as the soles of my feet.

"Sister Hannah is expecting me," I say.

Sister Hannah emerges as if on cue. Now that I see her close up, I have a better chance to assess her. I see her nun's habit, stained and torn in one spot. I see her gray eyes, kind but wary.

"I don't have extra room right now," she says.

I start talking nonetheless. Anything is possible if you use words in the right way. Lokure knew this when he insisted that I look at his letter. He knew that if I read it, I would not be able to cast aside his words, that they would burrow inside of me.

I open my mouth and let the words pour forth. "Every day that I go without being in school is a small death for me," I explain. "When I was a girl, I went to school every day. I never missed a day, except for once when I had malaria. I have to go to school, you see, not only for me, but for my mother, whom I presume to be dead. I have nothing left of my own. My one pair of earrings got torn right out of my ears, but I think that all I need is to get an education. Back in Kakuma, I met a woman inside the United Nations. She promised she would take me to you, but she never showed up, so I traveled here on my own. I am clever and good with my hands. I can help you. I can work hard."

My words come out in a jumble, one piling on top of the next. These words are not as beautiful as I would like them to be, and yet I continue to toss them into a heap at Sister Hannah's feet.

I see her pause. I am ready for her to wave me away but, incredibly, she does not tell me to "shoo."

She is a short heavy-set woman with impossibly pale skin. Her face is almost colorless, save her large black glasses. But, as my eyes roam downwards, I notice that her hands are gnarled and red, as if she has spent large amounts of time with them submerged in hot water.

"So the woman from the UN promised you a place here?" Sister Hannah asks. "And now you have come by yourself?"

I nod.

"Tell me, what is your name?"

"I have a good many names, but they call me Poni at present."

Sister's face seems to soften. "I have a saying. What God sends me, I don't turn away."

I should hold my tongue, but I can't. "But that other woman who came before me..."

"I have no time for beggars, not with so many people who are willing to work hard. You realize how many people come to my door every day? So I have to make some choices, yah. But clearly God has a mission for you. I can see it in your eyes." She looks at me sternly. "Tell me, young lady. Will you do as you claim and work hard?"

I look down at Sister Hannah's hands, those hands red with servility to God. "I will do good work. You will see this."

"Well, then, I will find space for you. I wasn't lying when I said we haven't any, but we will find a way." As if seeing my lack of comprehension, she adds, "I'm not going to send you away. Come in, please." She speaks in Kiswahili, then speaks in English with what I later learn is a German accent.

I cannot wait to walk inside with Sister, to possibly beg a bit of water to soothe my travel-parched mouth, and yet I am nervously looking behind me, as if expecting to find someone standing there.

So many people left behind, and yet me, I'm being saved. Let me not question my luck. Stop and examine good fortune for too long, and it might evaporate like water in the heat.

Without saying another word, I follow Sister Hannah into her compound. I am aware of my muddy feet, thin dress and lack of undergarments.

"Girls are safe here," Sister says, as if sensing my hesitation.

I nod. Little does she know that I am walking so slowly not because I don't wish to go inside — I have longed for such an invitation, have risked everything for it — but because I am saying goodbye to an entire chapter of my life, all those years spent in Kakuma. How long, precisely? How many years? One has no calendar in a refugee camp.

In Kakuma, time was a trickle of water pushing through cracked mud. Now, suddenly, things are moving once again.

—22—

SISTER BRINGS ME into her office and motions for me to sit in one of the chairs. It is an unfamiliar sensation, that of dropping onto a cushioned chair. I cross my ankles and sit up straight. Perhaps she is still deciding whether or not to keep me.

"So tell me exactly what it is you want here, Poni?" she asks me.

"Want?"

"You came to me to escape from Kakuma. You need food and clothing. I understand this quite well, but you also want more." Seeing that I am still confused, she continues, "I am able to help girls like you."

Looking at Sister's eyes, gentle but resolute, I think of all the things I do want. The list is long. To find Mama and my brothers, to hold my little sister and whisper life lessons in her ear, to locate the missing pages of a book, to rescue Tihou and Lokure.

But first things first.

"I want to continue my schooling."

Sister Hannah continues to look at me. She is a woman of God, a woman under whose gaze one cannot lie.

"I can help you, but you must follow my instructions exactly." Her voice turns terse. "I do not tolerate silliness here," she says. "Nor do I tolerate girls who take up with boys."

I nod. If only she knew about Lokure, about my turning my back on him in order to reach her.

"Of course, I make all my girls work. God values servitude, and there is certainly always much to be done here. Right now I have someone working with the elderly, but I need help in the orphanage. Can you cook?"

I think about Mama, about her lightning-fast fingers, the way she could chop vegetables into tiny pieces.

"I know how to cook," I tell her. It is true. I know from watching Mama all of those years, from tending the house even when Mama wasn't there.

"Safi," says Sister, who continues to pepper her sentences with Kiswahili. "You will cook and, if you do well, be given house duties." Unlike most of the missionaries I have met, who talk so quickly, Sister's voice is slow and deliberate, which is good since my English is poor.

"I am an old woman myself now, and I sometimes need assistance at night due to my asthma." She pauses. "You know what this is, asthma?" She does an impression of someone having trouble breathing.

"Ah, yes," I say. I talk with far more confidence than I actually have. "I am good with this. My father, he was a pharmacist."

She reaches out and pats me on the arm.

"Good girl," she says. "Don't be afraid. No men can come in from the outside. The guards watch the gate twenty-four hours." She looks at me and smiles. "You have arrived. You're one of the lucky ones." I smile back at her, but inside I feel strange. Like someone who is eating food while others are starving in the next room.

As I leave, I glance at the calendar that is sitting on Sister Hannah's desk. I quickly do the math in my head.

I am sixteen years old.

■■■

SISTER HANNAH HAS A Nuer girl named Nyanath show me to my room. This girl is very tall with tiny decorative scars encircling her mouth like fleshy beads.

"You will sleep in the room right next to Sister so that you can help her if she is having trouble breathing at night," she says.

I respond with "Maale," one of the only Nuer words I know. Nyanath gives me a tiny smile to hear a Didinga girl like me speak her language.

"Maale madit," she replies. There are a hundred questions I want to ask of this girl, but I remain silent. At least for now.

The room is small, barely big enough for the bed, with nothing on the walls but a simple metal cross hanging above my bed, but it is a real room with a bed, blanket and pillow.

I vow right here and now that I will do what I can to make Sister pleased with me. Unlike the UN woman who never showed up, I believe Sister can truly help me.

■■■

BEFORE I GO TO SLEEP that night, Sister comes to give me instructions. She is carrying a toddler whom she introduces as Paul.

"Someone found Paul abandoned near a pile of trash when he was only a few days old," she tells me. "I took him in and, together with the other girls, we saved his life. For days we kept him covered with blankets, gave him milk. We call him Kleine Paul, which means Little Paul in German."

I offer my hand to the little boy. "Then we shall be friends, for I, too, am sometimes called Paul." At this, the little boy smiles at me.

Sister instructs me. "At night I leave my door open, and you should do the same. That way you can hear me if I need help. I get malaria sometimes, like all of you," she says, "but this asthma is an additional thing. I have an inhaler by my bedside, but because I am old, I cannot always find my glasses in the middle of the night. I hope I'm not scaring you."

"That is one thing about me. I don't get scared."

Sister looks at me, as though she is studying me.

"Well, good. This is good."

That night I go to sleep under the cross. I think of Mama praying to this same cross all of those years. The thought of her being dead makes me hug myself as though I am a child.

Yet I am no longer one.

—23—

SISTER LIVES A HUMBLE life. She wakes every morning, prays and attends daily mass at the open-air church. She stays up late each night writing letters, going over finances, making lists of food and supplies.

There is no mirror in her room, no concession to vanity. And yet she does enjoy entertaining, especially to raise funds for the orphanage and other projects. Whenever she has a guest over, especially one from America or Germany, she laughs, charms, then gently plies the guest for money. "We are so low on supplies, you see," she confides. "May I show you around? Would you care to see the orphanage?" She enjoys visitors of all walks — missionaries, politicians and volunteers — those who enter from the outside world with tales of travel and politics.

On those nights when we have guests from Germany or the United States, I must work especially hard. Just when I sit down to eat a small amount of food that I have set aside for myself, I hear her calling me. "Poniiii." She lets the last part of my name trail off. "More tea for the guests," she says. And I appear, or sometimes I simply place the desired item in the service window between the kitchen and the dining room.

Just like Mama, who knew how to disappear when there were male guests in the home, I bring in the food and then, just as quickly, make myself invisible. Although Sister Hannah is always kind to us, she also expects us to know our place. She has us serve her the foods she likes — ravioli, chicken and potatoes — while we eat our ugali and sukamawiki in the kitchen.

When I'm not chopping or cooking in the kitchen, I assist the girls in the nearby orphanage. Some of the girls work with the elderly, helping them to feel comfortable. Others work in the orphanage like me, going up and down the rows of children. One of the little boys, whose mother died of AIDS, cries all the time, because he has sores all over his body.

"We have no good medicine," Sister tells us, "but something as simple as chamomile tea often does wonders."

That night, I take a cloth soaked in chamomile and pat it all over his body.

"It hurts," he says, gritting his small teeth together.

"I'll tell you what. I'll wash all this pain away," I tell him. I gently rub him down with the tea. After days of doing this, his skin does, in fact, heal.

Whenever Sister puts Paul down, we all take turns holding him. "You will make his head like this." Sister pantomimes a head growing as big as a ball, but we can see that she's secretly pleased. When the police brought Paul to Sister, no one thought he would survive. He was so little to be without a mother, and she did not know how long he had been lying outside by the trash. But now Paul is a healthy boy who is constantly getting passed around among us women.

"Our little man here will be growing up thinking he has twenty mothers," one of the girls says jokingly.

Paul asks Sister Hannah if she is his real mother. This despite the fact that Sister Hannah is nearly seventy, not to mention a nun and a white woman. The rest of the girls all begin to giggle until Sister tells us to hush.

Every night I sleep with my door open, waiting for Sister to call out to me. One night she does.

"Fräulein," she calls out. "Girl." In her half-groggy state, it is as though she has forgotten my name.

I appear by her bedside. "Sister, I'm here." I reach for her inhaler, just as she has instructed me to do. I put her glasses on and turn on the light by her bed. Luckily, the generator is working.

"I don't think I need the inhaler," she says. "But would you be so kind as to prop me up on my pillows. It is easier for me to breathe this way."

I have never seen her looking like this, her gray hair flowing across her shoulders, free of her habit. Her face is even whiter than usual.

"Would you like me to make you some tea, Sister?" I ask her.

"Just a little filtered water, Poni, please." Her voice is strained, but I am pleased to hear that she now knows me again. "Thank you. You have become my right-hand helper."

"You help so many people," I tell her. Then, without knowing why, I reach out and brush some hair away from her face.

"Good girl," she says.

I sit quietly with her, waiting for her breathing to return to normal.

After some time, she tells me, "You may go. I think I shall sleep soundly now."

Sister Hannah rejected a life of luxury. She chooses, instead, to live as we Africans do. She has a sister, Greta, who raises a good deal of money on our behalf, but Greta wears fancy clothes and lives in Germany. Sister Hannah, on the other hand, stays with us all the time and owns nothing. When people ask her why she stays, she says, "God whispered in my ear."

Nyanath told me that Sister once was attacked by street boys carrying guns. They charged into the compound, despite the guard out front. All Sister and the other girls could do was pray. The thieves took all of the money that Sister had hidden away in her office, money that was earmarked to buy supplies. Sister hired more guards following this event, but that was it. She still wouldn't leave.

■ ■ ■

I KNOW THAT SISTER always has much on her mind, so many people depending on her for their safety and well-being. However, even after I have worked for her for several months, she does not discuss my schooling. Every day I wake up wondering, is today the day she will finally send me to classes? After all, a few of the other girls already attend school.

I try to tell myself to be patient, but this is not my strength. I turn fidgety and restless. I develop a rash, one that is invisible to the eye but that makes me itch dreadfully.

Finally, I can stand it no longer. The trouble is, Sister is always occupied. One day, though, I see my opening, see Sister sitting by herself at her desk.

"Yes, Poni, you can approach," Sister says to me. "Tell me what you want, and then you and I will go over the dinner menu for tonight. I will have one of the guards accompany you into town to purchase supplies. We will serve ravioli, I think, blackcurrant juice, and House of Manji shortcake biscuits for dessert. Then, from the kiosk, we need Kimbo, Simba Mbili curry powder, Peptang, kiberiti, chevdo mix and Lucozade."

I take her list, but then suddenly, as I sit and squirm, trying not to scratch at the back of my legs, the words burst forth from my mouth.

"Sister, I am interested in continuing my schooling."

Sister stops what she is doing and looks at me. "Yes. Well, I did promise you this, didn't I? When you first came to see me?"

I try to read her thoughts. Does she consider me impudent?

"Of course you should go to school. I fear I have gotten so accustomed to you doing everything around here that I forgot to send you."

"I can still assist you in the evenings when I return," I tell her.

"Naturally," Sister says. "Give me another week or two, and we will get you started with classes." Then she adds, "Poni, you were right to say something to me. God provides everything, but what he overlooks we must seek out for ourselves. You must hold people to their promises."

"I know it is easy for you to get distracted. You look after so many people."

"And yet you notice I only take in those people who are also willing to help themselves."

I nod. I cannot explain it, but at this moment, it is as if we are sharing some type of secret. Sister is a humble servant of God, but she is also the first woman I have ever known who is really in charge of running her own business, if you can call our compound a business. Sister is the one who hires workers to construct new buildings when we need them. She is the one who oversees our water pump and the one who calls Kenya Power to complain when the electricity generator goes down for hours at a time. "Liars! Stupids!" she screams at the men on the phone if they try to tell her they will not be able to turn the generator on this day.

Sister's kindness is known all over Kenya, yet there is a steely determination about her as well. She comes from a tradition of old-school missionaries and is not a woman who is afraid to give orders, to bark them if need be.

As if confirming this fact, Sister points to some of the young orphan boys she sees urinating on the lawn.

"Animals! Bozibozi!" she yells out the window. "You are no longer in the camps. I have told you to use the toilet like proper boys."

■ ■ ■

SISTER STAYS TRUE TO HER word, and a few weeks later I begin classes at the all-girls secondary school. Slowly, my invisible rash leaves me, and I am able to sit still once again.

Imagine what it is like sitting in a real school. I sit up straight, my spine rigid, not wanting to miss a single word from the teacher. We sit on benches, wearing our red school uniforms, surrounded by white-washed walls. I have been given actual paper and pens but, being loath to waste these resources, I write with tiny letters. Occasionally, the electricity goes out, and when it does, our teacher turns on a big battery-operated lantern.

The teacher is an older man with tired eyes and hair that is gray only around his ears. He tells us that we must work extremely hard, that not everyone has our opportunity.

"Don't be under the false impression that all of you will pass this class," he warns. "Only the best students will rise to the top." I nod and try to send a mental message to this teacher. I will do whatever it takes to succeed at my studies. Lokure showed me all things are possible when he taught me to read in the dark.

I enter a happy yet exhausting routine. During the day I attend lectures, writing out my English exercises and memorizing historical dates, while during the evening I continue to assist Sister with cooking and organizing the stock room. Sister trusts me enough to hand over money to buy new supplies when needed. I do my writing exercises and read until I am holding my eyes open with my fingers.

Yet when I finally lie down in bed, just when you would think my brain would slow, my mind continues to run. Nighttime is when I picture Lokure bent over his porridge pot, the way his face lit up when he caught sight of me. As if this is not torture enough, I allow myself to recall the feeling of his tall-grass fingers against my cheek. I stroke my cheek with my own fingers, but it is not the same.

Sister has lived her entire life without the companionship of a man. She gave herself over to God instead.

For a long time, I thought marriage was a land mine. The notion that anyone would actually marry for love escaped me. But now when I think about Lokure, it is with the wistfulness of something lost. Remembering Lokure is like running a shard of glass down the inside of my arm.

You breathe through a memory. You make yourself forget.

—24—

IT IS DIFFERENT WAKING every day with a purpose, reawakening my mind that has slumbered for too long. When I have difficulty memorizing new facts, when I begin to pity myself, I think of Tihou and how envious she would be of my schooling. I wonder what became of her.

In school, I copy notes from the cracked chalkboard, writing so furiously and clutching my pen so hard that I grow a thick knot of skin on my middle finger. Groping my way around the English language forces my once-tattered tongue to move in all different directions, to form words that feel like something hard in my mouth.

A few nights a week, Nyanath, the Nuer girl, and I work in the orphanage. Our task is feeding the babies and placing the children in their beds. Rows and rows of children who will grow up in Sister's compound, not knowing that they came from Sudan, not remembering that they once had real mothers who risked their lives in hot birthing huts in order to squeeze them out into the world.

Yet these children do not spend their days sad. They have learned how to care for one another. Even the little ones know how to quiet those children who suffer from bad dreams at night. Big girls carry around little girls, and little girls carry around even smaller girls. They fashion jump ropes out of spare string and toy cows out of the clay they find by digging in the dirt.

I am always busy, but during the rare moments when I do have free time, I try to tell the children stories. I tell the story of how the tortoise got its shell, and I tell them how the cricket got its song.

When the children demand more food, and we do not have any extra to spare, I remember Mama's trick of making a small amount of food seem like more.

"Would you like one piece of mango or five?" I ask the children.

"Oh, five, five!" they all yell, and so I cut the mango into very tiny pieces. "There you are. Five pieces for every child. You didn't think I would be able to give you so much, did you?" They nod happily, not noticing that the pieces are smaller.

■ ■ ■

YOU WOULD THINK THAT all of us girls would bond together out of solidarity. We are the lucky few who have survived. Yet when there is not enough firewood or grain to go around, something in you changes. You begin to view even your friends as competitors.

Sister Hannah tells us, "I don't care whether your tribes were friendly or hostile with one another in Sudan. Here inside my compound you will treat one another respectfully. If not, I will provide you with a ticket and send you back to Kakuma. I will say goodbye and wish you well. Do you understand? This is a no-war zone, girls."

"Yes, Sister," we all intone.

"We, all of us, pray to the same God. We, all of us, are victims of the same war."

"Yes, Sister."

"Girls, you must always act in a respectable way. You know what I mean by this. I expect you to act like ladies. God expects this, too. Please feel my eyes on you at all times. Like God's eyes, they are the eyes of judgment. If you do something, I want you to ask yourself, 'Would Sister approve of my behavior?' If the answer is no, then you shouldn't do it. Guard yourselves, girls. Don't be misled by boys."

"Yes, Sister."

"You girls are the lucky ones. You must do well, and then you must return and help your mothers, aunties and elders back home. You must return and help the weak ones."

"Yes, Sister."

I look around at the girls who now surround me, the other girls Sister Hannah has saved. I should try to make friends with them, should ask to study with the ones from my classes. Yet something holds me back.

I hear the words of our teacher. "Not all of you will pass the class." By helping others, will I hurt my own chances at success? Perhaps it is safer to trust no one.

Sister does her best to maintain peace among us girls, to insist that we show gratitude, that we thank God and pray to him.

"Without God we are nothing," she repeats daily. "Let us pray for peace."

And yet we girls know an unfortunate secret. Peace only works on paper.

It seems I am not the only girl who is distrustful. The other girls find ways to sabotage one another. But they do it carefully, so that Sister Hannah cannot catch them. Aduei, a girl with an antelope face, constantly treads on my heels when she walks behind me.

When I turn to give her a sharp look, she says, "Oh, it was an accident." But I know the truth.

Other girls yank one another's skirts when Sister's back is turned.

They gossip, too. "Do you see how ugly that one is," a group of girls says, pointing to the girl named Josephine. "Her eyes are two different sizes. She has the eyes of a frog."

"Are you girls whispering?" Sister Hannah snaps.

"No, Sister."

The girls are quiet in front of Sister Hannah. They are afraid of her. Still, they know that she cannot understand them very well when they switch into their own native dialects. This is how they continue their bickering, smiling brightly at Sister while secretly insulting one another in their own tongues.

Growing up in the villages, everything was shared. If you had a piece of bread, you always broke it in two. However, the war destroyed this communal way of thinking and taught us to be for ourselves.

Perhaps this is why I feel so lonely. I am surrounded by girls, but I have no friends.

There is one exception. I end up gravitating to the girl with the personality most opposite from my own.

During our time together in the orphanage, Nyanath and I talk to one another. Despite Nyanath's beauty, there is something unassuming about her. Her posture is perfectly straight, and her voice is always slow and deliberate, as if she is trying to subdue those around her.

If my personality is white, frothy waters, Nyanath's is a calm lake. Being a town girl, I know the date when I was born, but Nyanath, who comes from a small village near Bentiu, does not know her actual age. "Oh, I am somewhere between twenty and twenty-three," she says when people ask her.

"Nyanath, why don't you attend classes like some of the other girls?"

"I already know I'm going to become a nun," she tells me. "God already has a plan for me."

"But don't you still want to pursue your education?" I ask.

"I don't need any studies except for the Bible."

"You are satisfied reading this same book over and over again?"

Nyanath looks at me. "I think you ask a great deal of questions."

"So I've been told."

I am drawn to Nyanath's peacefulness, and yet I also want to shake her. How is she so calm all the time? So satisfied?

"Why are the girls here so mean to one another?"

Nyanath thinks about it and then says, "These girls have forgotten how to behave. They were in the refugee camp too long. They forgot what it was like to have parents or town elders."

"But not you?"

"No. I have not forgotten."

"Sometimes I wonder if we'll ever have a home to return to."

"God is your home, and he moves with you wherever you go." I nod, but I wish I was convinced. I don't dare confess to Nyanath how restless I feel most of the time. I worry she might accuse me of being ungrateful.

Nyanath is the other girl to whom Sister Hannah entrusts the most important house duties. Because Nyanath is always at the compound, she is also privy to many pieces of news, yet when she conveys them she does so without being gossipy.

During the rest time between our chores, Nyanath asks me, "Poni, are you thinking of leaving Africa like some of the other girls?"

"Some girls are leaving?" This takes me by surprise.

"Sister says there are better education opportunities in other countries."

"Like where?"

"There are countries that will sponsor you. The most likely ones are Canada, Australia or the United States."

"Sister never mentioned the possibility of leaving to me."

"Sister only wants what is good for all us girls. You know this. But, I personally think that sometimes she gets attached to some people and wants them to stay."

That night, as I go to sleep, my mind spins with the possibility of leaving Africa. I can picture the map my teacher pulled out when I was a schoolgirl. I remember being astounded that such a large world existed. Yet Africa is the only life I've ever known.

—25—

EVERY DAY THE GUARDS who stand outside Sister's compound have to shoo away the men who gather there. Some of the men pretend to be our uncles.

"Please," they call out. "My brother's daughter is inside the compound. I've come to fetch her."

Do these men really think that we will be tricked in this way? Do they really expect us to go to them?

Sister is not intimidated. She goes out and tells the guards to "make sure these men do not loiter." Then she shouts, in less-than-godly terms, that if they do not leave, she will have them arrested. Though Sister is a short woman, she can puff herself up and appear larger than her real size.

"Stupids!" she yells at the men, her insult of choice.

Though I do go to the marketplace in Nairobi or Thika on Saturdays to buy food for Sister, I mostly remain within the Juja compound. Unlike Kakuma, Sister's compound is no holding cell, but it is still a waiting place. With the exception of Nyanath, most of us girls are impatient, thinking about what our futures will bring.

I try to force loneliness down my throat. I have swallowed far worse — water mixed with mud, mosquitoes, grass and bitter leaves. Why then can I not swallow this? At night, with no one looking, I run my hands across my body under the covers. I feel my chest ache with a longing I cannot place.

Did I miss my one chance to be loved when I left Lokure? Will anyone ever long after my tattered body again?

■■■

AT SCHOOL I CONTINUE to study as though my life depends on it. And doesn't it? "Not all of you girls will make it." This is what the instructor warned. I write lists of English words over and over again until I commit them to memory. When I have no paper left, I continue to write on my hands, my arms.

Sometimes, when I don't need to serve food at the compound, I skip my meals and study instead. Going without food, denying my body's appetites, is something I am already good at. Eating is always the first thing I cut out when I am busy. In fact, now that I am no longer starving, keeping a small amount of sharpness in my stomach feels good and familiar.

One day when I am attending classes, our teacher tells us that he has received several boxes of books donated by a Catholic organization.

"Please feel free to look through the collection and tell me if you wish to borrow a book. Some are meant for children, but some might be appropriate for your age group."

After class, I eagerly approach the boxes of books and begin to look through them. One of the books has a man and a woman on the front locked in a passionate embrace.

The man wears no shirt, and the woman has long flowing yellow hair and a dress that is open to reveal most of her breasts. I quickly put this book down.

Then I see it. It is Chinua Achebe's *Things Fall Apart*. I hardly believe my eyes.

I know what Nyanath would say. "It's a sign, Poni."

I approach my teacher. "Sir, may I borrow this book?"

"Ah," my teacher looks pleased. "A fine choice, Poni. Yes, I'll write down your name, and you may take it with you. Just return it when you've finished."

"If you only knew how long I have searched for this." I take the book and cradle it.

"You're a good student, Poni. Enjoy."

That night I rush through my chores so that I can go to my room and begin reading. Unlike Kakuma, where I had to read in the dark, here at Sister Hannah's my eyes do not have to perform magic. I read without stopping, without looking up, read until the room fades away around me.

Finally I reach the ending of the book — the real ending this time. It feels wrong to read it before Lokure has the chance.

When I last left off reading Achebe's book, missionaries had arrived in the Igbo village. I knew that the main character's death was inevitable as soon as he decided to try to fight the missionaries. Yet when I reach the end of the book and see that I was right, I still feel devastated.

I had hoped that reading Achebe's book and its long-awaited ending would fill me up, leave me satiated. Instead it leaves me hungrier than ever. I know I will need more than this one book.

■ ■ ■

BACK IN KAKUMA, people always whispered about America. Here at Sister Hannah's the girls do the same thing. Some speak of "a land of opportunity."

Others speak of danger.

"America will eat you alive, then spit you out."

"Do you know that Americans have so much money that they hire people to brush their dogs' teeth?"

"These people are called millionaires, and they are everywhere in America."

"In America, people have more than one bathroom in their house. Sometimes they have ten bathrooms in one house. Maybe they go and pee into each one."

"They have schools everywhere in America. You can choose which school you want to go to. There are schools for everyone, and girls are told to go to school there, just like the boys."

I don't know which of these rumors to believe, but suddenly, I do know that I must find out the truth for myself.

I don't know how, but I must get to this country.

■ ■ ■

THE NEXT DAY, I APPROACH Sister yet again. She is in her office screaming out the window at the workers. "You have not placed the barbed wire as I told you. Pull it out and start once more!"

Sister is in a dark mood. This much is clear. I try to back out of the doorway, but it is too late. She has already spotted me.

"I give them instructions, but they go about things however they choose, willy-nilly."

"Sister, there is something — "

"What? Out with it." She doesn't give me time to dance around the question at hand.

I say my words quickly, so that I won't have time to reconsider them.

"I think I need to go to America, to continue my studies. I think I can find more books there."

Sister pauses and takes off her glasses. She acts as though she was waiting for just such a request.

"Well, in fact, your timing is perfect. I am actually working on sending a group of girls over to America, but I didn't think you wanted to go."

"I am told I might go to a university in America."

Will she tell me that I'm being foolish?

Instead, she simply says, "Yes, well, I think this is a highly sensible choice for you." She nods, as if this has decided it. "So since you're interested, I'll explain. An organization called the African Center places girls in various destinations around the United States — South Dakota, Minnesota, upstate New York. All cold states for some reason. But I have to warn you, this sponsorship process is very slow and tough."

"That's all right," I tell her. "I can handle all this." What could be tougher than what I have already been through?

"Poni, whatever you have heard about the United States, life isn't easy there. As a refugee, you have to work five times harder than other people."

I nod. Perhaps I should be frightened but, as always, I am too foolish to be.

■ ■ ■

WHEN THE GIRLS ARE not cooking, cleaning or studying, they gather around a small television in the gray common room.

"This is what America is like," they say, pointing to the television. They watch *Walker, Texas Ranger*.

"You should come watch with us, Poni," they say.

Instead, I open my book of English words and, as I do every night, I drag my tongue over these words, forcing them to fit within my teeth.

■ ■ ■

A FEW DAYS LATER, Sister gathers several of us girls together. "I'm going to start arranging for you to do interviews through the commission for refugees. I don't mean to scare you, but you get only one chance at this. If you fail your interview, you don't get an opportunity to interview again for many years, if at all."

Wait more years? Add this to the years we have already wasted, and I realize that failing the interview is not an option. My girlhood has already dried up. I simply cannot lose any more years.

■ ■ ■

OVER THE NEXT COUPLE of weeks, Sister works with us to prepare us for our interviews.

"You must write your essays in advance, my girls. You must tell this commission why you should go to the United

States. You must prove that you are fleeing persecution."

Sister looks right at one of the girls, Rose Lolik. Rose has a habit of tilting her head towards her shoulder to hide the large scar down her face. I have never asked about how she came by this scar. Girls do not reveal the things that happened to them when their villages were attacked or when they were in Kakuma. Girls speak in code. "Things happened," a girl might be heard to whisper. Many of the girls were raped, either by soldiers, guards or foster parents. Many of the girls were beaten or worse. But they do not speak of it. To what end?

Sister Hannah speaks to Beatrice. "I know you don't like to look people in the eye. This is natural for you Sudanese, but in America it means you are lying. If the person interviewing you thinks you are avoiding his eyes, you fail the test. You must overcome your fear, Beatrice."

"Okay," Beatrice replies. Her voice is gravelly and burnt-sounding.

"Oh, and Beatrice, you need to speak more loudly," Sister informs her. "Pretend you are speaking to someone in the back of the room, and please remember to shake hands when you greet someone."

At this, Beatrice looks completely embarrassed, but she says, "I understand," much more loudly.

Kuir, another girl, asks, "Sister, if the commission people are asking for information such as our age or when this or that happened, what should we tell them? There is so much I don't remember."

Sister takes Kuir's hands. "This is really the problem, girls. The commission wants you to have an answer for everything. If the person interviewing you thinks you are lying or thinks your story is unclear, they will reject you. You must fill in the facts you don't remember. Do you understand what I am telling you? It's not that I am advising you to lie, but you must make reasonable guesses. God will forgive these small transgressions," she continues. "Think about it from the point of view of the interviewer. You are trying to become a refugee, to prove that you cannot stay in your homeland, so is the interviewer going to want to hear that you've had a simple, easy life?"

All of us girls look at one another as if to confirm the obvious and then shake our heads.

"You Sudanese women are taught not to speak about your problems, but for the interviews, you need to tell. Many of the boys going to America are getting famous by sharing their stories. But what about you girls?"

"Shall I tell them that my parents were both killed?" Beatrice asks.

"Yes, but girls, do you know how many hundreds of applicants will have this same story? Who in the camps hasn't lost a mother, father or brother? You need to make your story different, need to make it unique. Do you understand? When you write your essay, you need to include description. You only get this one chance, see?"

That night, I lie in bed trying to think of how to share my life experience with a stranger. Must I reopen all the images of death and destruction that I keep rolled up and tied with reeds?

Bad things happened to us girls. Has it come down to who can describe them the best?

I have long since used up all of the words that Lokure gave me. It is up to me to find my own words now.

■ ■ ■

ONE DAY AS WE ARE sitting at the lunch table, I see Rose
Lolik gazing intently at a piece of paper she is holding. It
seems she has forgotten to tilt her head, as she usually does
to hide her scar. I look at this scar, which runs from just below her eye to the bottom of her cheek, thorny as an acacia
branch. What memories does Rose keep within this jagged
piece of skin?

Rose, sensing my gaze upon her, turns towards me. I
think she will talk to me, but instead she clicks her tongue.

"Why are you eyeing me?"

Her question catches me off guard. I start to speak, but
Rose doesn't give me the chance. She starts waving the paper she is holding in front of me.

"Are you trying to steal this?"

Now I am confused. "Steal what? That piece of paper?"

"You can't have this, Poni. No one can." I am completely surprised to hear Rose yelling like this. Rose, who usually ducks her head, who hardly ever speaks.

Even though I don't know why she's carrying on this
way, I reach out my hand to try to calm her. She doesn't
take it. Instead she runs out of the room.

I look over at Nyanath, utterly bewildered. "What just
happened?"

"It is not your fault. The paper she carries. It's the address of a white volunteer Rose met in Kakuma. She carries
it with her everywhere. She thinks that if she gets to America, she will find this person, and he will help her."

Does Rose really hate me so much that she thinks I
would steal this from her? Has it come to this?

But then I think of Rose's face. Things were done to girls. Best to hide things away, whether it is the address of a volunteer or a thorny scar across your face. Hide it where no one else can find it.

I hope Rose does make it to America. Truly, I hope her volunteer does save her.

If only she knew this. If only I could tell her.

■■■

THE FOLLOWING NIGHT Nyanath moves nearby as I am hunched over my paper, trying to write another draft of my essay.

"I hear you may be leaving soon," she tells me.

"I'm trying," I tell her. "Will you come, too? Will you fill out the necessary paperwork?"

"Some girls are meant to leave. My place is here with Sister Hannah."

"I don't know how I'll make it without you, Nyanath, without you calming me all the time."

"You'll survive," she says with a smile. "Don't worry. I think God has good fortune in store for both of us."

Nyanath is the only one who believes this. That there is no limit on good luck, that there is enough to go around.

■■■

FINALLY, THE DAY for my commission interview arrives. Despite my earlier claim that I am fearless, I wake up with my whole body numb from nerves.

The interview starts at 8:30 a.m. sharp. Although Nairo-

bi is only nineteen miles from Juja, the roads have so many
deep holes that we must allow ourselves three hours for the
journey. Sister Hannah tells me that Americans work by
the clock and that if we are late for our interview, we will
lose our chance.

"If you are even five minutes late, you're done. There
are too many other people lined up for them to wait on
you," she tells us.

We are about six miles away from the interview when our
car gets stuck in the mud. All of us girls look at one another.

This cannot be happening, not now.

The driver gets out. He signals that Sister Hannah
should press her foot on the gas pedal while he pushes. The
car's tires spin, but every time they do, they seem to drive
the car even deeper into the mud.

"Stupid!" Sister Hannah yells, this time to the car.

Meanwhile, the driver kicks at the wheels and curses.
Then, remembering the nun in his presence, he apologizes
profusely. But Sister Hannah is not interested in anything
but the time.

"Get out and walk, girls. Hurry." I can hear the panic in
her voice. "You've no time to spare. I'll stay behind with
the driver. You can't be late, girls, so go."

I picture an American man waiting to interview me. See
him look at his clock and, when I am late, get up to leave. I
want to scream out to him, to tell him to wait.

The hard voice in my head taunts me again. *So many
girls left behind, and you thought you could escape.*

But I ignore the voice once more and do what I do best.
I run without waiting or looking to see whether or not the
other girls are with me.

I am a little girl again, running while people fall down around me.

Something is trying to pull me back. This time it is the mud on the road, thick and clingy as despair. The mud grabs at anything it can get to — my shoes, the hem of my dress — but still I keep going.

Sweat trickles down my back and into my undergarments. Will I ever get to stop running?

The interviewer with the clock is waiting for me. America, this strange country, is waiting for me. That is if it doesn't close its doors before I have a chance to get there.

I am panting now, gasping for breath. But then I look up and, like a beacon in front of me, I see the sign for the high commissioner's building.

I look around to see if any of the other girls are with me, worried that I have lost them for good. But then I see them. They are a ways behind me, but they are coming. I begin to laugh with relief to see them panting and plowing towards me: Rose Lolik, Kuir, Beatrice, Grace Choi.

"This way," I yell, pointing towards the sign. "This way, girls."

We have made it this far. Now come the interviews.

Who will make it farther still?

■■■

WHEN I GET INSIDE, my mouth is so dry from running, but I don't dare ask for water. I sit down and wait to be called. My legs tremble, but I cannot tell whether it is from nerves or from the running. I move my tongue around my mouth, try to make it wet enough so that I can at least speak. My tongue, once split and tattered, must work, must now win me a spot in America.

The white man who is assigned to interview me is dressed in a dark suit and has a face that reveals no emotion. I look down at my own muddy dress hem, but I don't try to explain it or tell the man about our car breaking down. Sister Hannah told us that Americans don't like excuses.

"I am going to turn the recorder on now," my interviewer says. "Try to just answer the questions I ask you."

"Yes, sir," I reply. Is it sir? Is this the correct title? I remember Sister Hannah's instructions. *Look him in the eyes. Cast-down eyes could mean that you are lying. You must go with the American way now.*

"Your age?"

"I am eighteen years old."

Say your answers with conviction. Do not act as though you have any doubts.

"How many brothers and sisters do you have?"

I remind myself that he is referring to brothers and sisters in the strict sense of the word.

"I have three."

"Any alive?"

"Not that I know of."

"Your mother?"

"I believe she's dead."

"Your father?"

"I believe he's dead."

"Did you see any of them killed?"

"Not with my own eyes."

"But you think they're dead?"

"Yes."

"Tell me about the night you fled your village."

Use descriptions. "It was very dark, but I still saw things." *Be specific.* "I saw my neighbor bending over her foot, because a bomb had taken it." *Use all of your senses to describe what happened.* "My ears — I couldn't hear out of one ear because the bombs were so loud. But even so, I could hear people screaming. I smelled hair burning, the sourness of blood. I am sorry, sir, to speak of such things, but since you asked. I lost my mother and my sister in the chaos. We were all running at once. There was a woman running with a child on her back, but the child had no head on it. Both child and mother were killed moments later by a bomb."

"How did you get to Kakuma?"

"I walked. We all walked across the desert. My tongue was dry enough as to split down the middle, and people were sitting down all around me to die. So many different kinds of deaths, the soft ones, the loud ones. There was a white Land Rover that got hit by a land mine. Everyone dead. Bodies everywhere."

I stop and look at my interviewer. His face is so blank.

What is he thinking? How many of these stories has he heard, and how is mine any different?

"Do you feel your life is still in danger?"

"Yes. I can't go back to my village, since it was destroyed. There are men who wait outside Sister Hannah's compound and say they are our uncles. They threaten to steal us away and force us into marriage."

"I see," he says.

Does he see? Does he believe me? I see the pink of his ears, see how he swats at flies like a foreigner, but there is no sign of concern on his face. My story is every story he has already heard. We all of us walked. We all of us saw people die. Why should he help me? Help one person, and a hundred more appear with their hands outstretched.

In telling him my story, I am pulling out bits of myself, handing them over like offerings. Yet he only needs the bad parts of my life. He does not want to hear about the mangoes, the laughter. He does not want to hear that my childhood was a happy one, that everyone in my village had eyes on me, that there was no such thing as a closed door.

But I am willing to leave it all behind for a country I know nothing about.

As if reading my thoughts, the interviewer asks, "Why do you want to go to America?"

"It's a place where I can get better schooling." Should I show him the knot of skin on my finger? Tell him how hard I have studied?

"In school, I am always first in my class. But I have run out of books to read here. I have dreams, you see, of going to America. Then one day I might be able to return and bring peace to Sudan."

"Thank you," the interviewer says. "You will hear back from us in a few months' time."

That's it? It is over? "There is more that I can tell you if you need — "

"No. I have everything." He nods at me and gets up. I practice the handshake Sister Hannah has taught me. The man's hand is smooth on the inside, soft and unwrinkled, so different from the red, gnarled hands of Sister Hannah. I watch him gather his recording machine and notes, then leave the room with his black leather bag slung over his shoulder. A bag containing countless stories, each story representing a life just like my own.

My fate rests in that black bag of his.

■ ■ ■

WEEKS PASS. Surely I know better than to get my hopes up. Though I was able to reach Sister's on my own, I cannot go to America without help. I cannot walk and swim that far. There is nothing to do but wait.

I have been waiting for half of my life, but this new wait is unbearable.

■ ■ ■

IT IS, IN FACT, Nyanath who knocks on my door weeks later to tell me that the commission has contacted Sister. She does not leave me in suspense for very long.

"Will you still remember me when you go to America?"

"Are you making a joke or have I really been selected?"

"Poni, you know I have no sense of humor. Do you know where Colorado is?"

"No," I say, still in shock.

"Sister says it is near mountains. They are just like the Didinga Hills, so you'll feel at home there."

"The Rocky Mountains? But my primary teacher showed me these on a map many years ago," I say excitedly.

"You see. It was a prophecy," Nyanath replies.

■ ■ ■

WHEN SISTER SEES ME, she immediately motions me in.

"Ah, Poni. You have heard the news from Nyanath? You must be so pleased. What's more, we have already secured a place for you at the university, and they will even give you student housing."

The thought of getting to attend an American university fills me with absolute awe. I have no idea what to expect. I wonder whether Americans do have a toilet in every single room of their house.

"Wait until you see the library at the university, Poni. You've never seen so many books."

I know I should feel nothing but happiness, but for some reason it still seems as though there is a weight on my chest, making it hard for me to breathe.

"What about the other girls?"

"Most are still waiting to hear. But don't worry. Your going to America will give the other girls hope." I nod, but inside, I feel so heavy.

How can I tell her that being someone else's hope feels like too great a burden to bear?

"Remember when you first showed up here? You told me how hard you would work, and you did, Poni. You made everything happen for yourself."

I want to tell Sister everything, want the stones removed from my chest.

"God sees everything. Right, Sister?"

"He does."

"I told lies to get here..." I cannot finish. But Sister does not need for me to.

"God sees, but he understands. I believe he understands

everything, even the not-so-pretty things people do to survive. Most important, he forgives."

"I'm scared, Sister," I tell her. It is the first time I have ever uttered these words. "My mother is dead, but she is still here in Africa somewhere. How can I leave her behind?"

Sister pauses. "There is this American children's movie. I saw it in Germany when I was young. It's called *Bambi*. Do you know it?"

I shake my head.

"It's the story of a deer, a deer like the ones we have here in Africa. One day hunters come, so the deer and his mother have to run away. Do you know what the mother deer says to Bambi as they are running for their lives?"

I shake my head.

"She says, 'Don't look back. Keep running.' Yes, you see, the mother wants him to keep moving to safety away from the hunters."

"And does he make it?"

"He does." Then she adds, "But his mother doesn't."

"The mother dies?" I'm surprised to hear that children's movies are so sad in America.

"She does. I remember crying at this part."

"But what does this mean?"

"You must look forward, not backward. You see?"

I nod. "I think so."

"Good. Go now, Poni," she says with a smile.

I get up to leave, but then I turn back. I forgot to tell Sister how much I will miss her, how much I owe her. But when I start to open my mouth, I see that she is already bent over her notebook, working. I quietly walk away.

■ ■ ■

THAT EVENING, as I am walking to my room, I hear someone sobbing. I look, and there is Grace Choi huddled in the hallway, curled against the wall.

"Grace? What has happened?"

"I did not pass my interview," she says, her back still to me.

I kneel down next to her. "But why?" Grace Choi has five children whom she cares for all by herself. If anyone deserves to go to America, it is Grace and her children.

"Even though my husband disappeared, I cannot prove he is dead. I don't qualify as an unattached minor or something like this."

I put my arms around Grace, feel her body vibrating with tears and disappointment. It is the first time any of the girls here has allowed me to touch her.

After a few moments, she collects herself and looks at me. "And you, Poni? Have you heard back from the commission?"

I stare for a long moment and then simply shake my head.

One last lie. I think about Sister's words, about how God forgives.

■ ■ ■

THAT NIGHT, I HAVE a dream. I am trying to flee my village and have arrived, once again, at the river. As I try to swim to safety, human arms emerge from the river. These hands pull at me from all sides, try to claim me, drag me under.

Suddenly, I take out the long black whip made of rhinoceros skin that the elders used during my brother's initiation rite. I start to whip at these arms. The cracking is too loud, and I want to cover my ears but I cannot. Thrash, thrash. I see the arms shrivel away under the impact of the blows I give them. Thrash, thrash. Yet some of these arms grow back, regenerate as quickly as I can destroy them.

I do not stop. I keep whipping, whipping, until finally I have reached the other side. I run and run until I trip on a tree root and fall to the ground. The sensation of landing with a jolt is what wakes me up.

I sit upright, disoriented.

Where am I? I am in my bed, but what woke me? Does Sister need me? Is she having trouble with her breathing? But as I listen, all is quiet. I hear the sound of Sister's soft snoring across the hall, the dogs barking outside. When I look up, I see the familiar cross above my bed.

All is calm.

■■■

BACK IN KAKUMA, I felt time had ground to a halt. Now it feels like events are happening too quickly.

Sister Hannah receives a computer from her sister in Germany, and all at once, we can access the Internet. I can hardly believe it when I learn that there is actually a Southern Sudanese chat site. Naturally, all the girls line up to use this site. Many of the girls are hoping to locate lost relatives or hear news of their villages back home. Sister Hannah shows me how to create a password and log myself on.

It turns out that there are hundreds of Southern Sudanese people who post messages on this site — messages in which they try to find one another or to talk about Sudanese politics.

Suddenly, it is as though hundreds of voices, unheard for so long, are all trying to tell their stories at once. A desperate chorus.

On a sudden impulse, I add my own post. *I am Zenitra Lujana Paul Poni, about to relocate to Colorado, where I will begin studies at the university.* Then I add, *I am alive.*

—26—

THREE DAYS MORE until I fly to America. Sister Hannah has helped me register online for classes at the university. These classes have strange names: *The Politics of War and Peace, Women's Gender Empowerment, Rap Music as Social Commentary.*

Will I be able to understand the classes themselves, much less their names?

At night, before I go to sleep, I check the Sudanese chat site once more.

Once I start, it is hard to stop reading all of the messages people have posted, all of the back-and-forth debates:

We must forgive the SPLA soldiers. During times of war, bad things happen, and there is no sense blaming those who are fighting for our cause.
Signed, Parek Bul.

Would you forget those who abused your aunt and burnt your hut? No. These men who do bad things go against their own people. I am not willing to forgive.
Signed, Lam Kuol.

*Southern Sudan will one day stand as an independent
country. We will wait for this new country.
Signed, Eliakim Akol.*

*I am still in the camp. We have only one blanket which
we have torn into two pieces to share. It is not enough.
Do not forget us here.
Signed, Margaret Hasaan.*

I make myself read through the death announcements,
like doing penance. This one killed in town violence, this
one dead from malaria, this one killed by a bullet wound,
this one's whereabouts unknown. I look for names of my
family members and am both frustrated and relieved when
I do not find any. I look at the list of refugees who have
been resettled in the United States, in places like South Dakota, Nebraska, Minnesota — states that, until recently, I
had never heard of.

Then, suddenly, I read a message that nearly stops my
heart.

Poni? It is me, your cousin Keiji.

It is as though a hand from the past has reached out to
grab me. Keiji? Could this really be my cousin Keiji with
her fluttery butterfly laugh? Keiji who braided my hair
and giggled as she handed me the love letter from Lokure
so many years ago? I can picture her, her smile. I want to
scream out with joy.

But then I read the rest of the message.

Poni, if this is really you, I need to tell you that I am
here with your mother. You must phone me right away.

Suddenly the room begins to spin around me. I grab the
wall, feeling as though my legs might give way. I am afraid
I might become ill.

Mama?

I run to Sister Hannah's office. I can barely enter Keiji's
phone number with my fingers shaking so badly. It feels as
though I have entered a dream, one in which my fingers
and feet are no longer my own.

The phone rings, and then a female voice answers. Time
stops.

"Keiji?" Is it really her? It doesn't sound like her.

"Who is this?" The voice is suspicious.

"Me, Poni."

Another long pause. Then, finally, "So it is true. You are
truly alive. Yes, this is your cousin Keiji."

"Where are you? Where is Mama?" It is as though I cannot ask her the questions quickly enough, as though I can
barely breathe.

"Cairo, Egypt. It has been a long journey to get here, but
please know that I am here living with your mother, Mama
Nahoyen, and several others." Keiji's voice has gotten flat
over the years. I remember Mama calling Keiji foolish so
long ago. Gone is Keiji's laugh now, replaced by something
dull. Things happened to so many girls.

"All these years I thought Mama was dead. Let me speak
with her." My heart is pumping so hard, I can feel it in my
ears.

There is a long pause. "Well, I didn't want to tell

you by e-mail. Your mama is alive, but she is very ill."

"Ill? In what way? I have to speak with her." My voice is now pleading, that of a child.

"She is very weak, has stopped eating. She goes in and out of sleep a great deal."

"Have you taken her to a doctor?"

"We took her. They said she has a bad infection of the blood and sent us home with medicine. The doctor wanted her to stay in the hospital, but she refused. She doesn't trust this doctor, and neither do I."

"Is Mama dying?" Keiji would know. After seeing so many people die around us, we have all of us gotten good at identifying those ready to depart this world.

Keiji does not answer my question directly. Instead she speaks in that dispirited voice of hers, "When can you come to Egypt? If you come soon you might be able to see her before God takes her." Though I cannot see Keiji's face, I know that the cousin I once knew is gone.

"Come to Egypt? Right now?" My mind is whirring. How can I do this? Yet if what Keiji is saying is true, this may be my only chance to see Mama alive. There is so much I want to ask her, so much I want to tell her. Mostly, I just want to touch her. "Keiji, I'm leaving for America in a few days' time. I am going to start taking classes at the university there."

"So for a university, you would turn your back on your mother?" Her words are scorpion bites.

"Keiji, please, put Mama on the phone. Even if she cannot speak to me, she can listen. I need her to hear my voice."

"Poni, she might not know you anymore, might think you a ghost."

"Please, please bring the phone to her ear. I'm begging you."

"Okay. I am bringing the phone to her," Keiji says after a long pause.

"Mama?" There is no response. I try to listen for her breathing, but the connection is not that good. "Mama, it is me, Poni." I picture Mama, remember the time when she sat by my bedside while I recovered from malaria, remember her praying over me. "Mama?"

Still no answer. Not knowing what to do, I suddenly begin chanting the names of all of my ancestors. I chant and chant, but then I stop because all at once I hear Mama's voice.

It is quiet, but it is unmistakably hers. "Chi Chi?"

Upon hearing my nickname, I cannot contain the tears. For so long in Kakuma, I was too dry to produce any water, but now I am crying so hard that I am drowning. Tears are running into my ears and down my face.

Still I try to speak, to tell her everything. "I ran so fast that night, Mama, I didn't know that I wouldn't see you again, that so much time would pass. Did you tell me to run, Mama? Did you tell me to run and not look back?"

Mama does not reply, but simply begins to sing:

Quiet, baby. Don't cry, baby.
Mama will come bring you milk fresh from the cow.

It is the song she used to sing to me when I was a child. The song is everything at once. The mango trees, the Kinyeti River covering every part of me, my ears, my nose, my eyes. This song threatens to pull me under.

Is this God's final test of me?

What should I do? I could go to Egypt. Yet if I do this I will sacrifice everything: my chance to go to America, my placement at the university. How long will it be before I am given another chance? A semester? A year? What if I never get this chance again?

"I have an opportunity to go to America, to continue my studies, but now that I know you are alive, I can't leave you behind. Tell me what to do, Mama. I am begging you. If you tell me not to go, I won't."

I wait to hear my mother's voice, but she is silent again.

I remember Mama lifting her dress above her knees, making me run my fingers across the scars. Those scars felt like small roads.

Maybe all this time she was preparing me for this moment when I would have to take a different path from hers, when I would have to leave her behind for good.

Suddenly, I know what I must do. It feels as though someone is squeezing my heart.

"I love you, Mama," I say softly.

When Keiji takes the phone back again, she says, "You will come see your mother?"

"No. I can't come, Keiji. The university ... it's the only chance I have."

"I see. Well, perhaps you can send money for the funeral, then."

Keiji's words have their desired effect. They rob me of my breath.

"Keiji, please take care of my mother. Put any anger you have towards me aside, and don't let her die alone."

"She is my auntie, and I'll care for her like I would my

own mother. Unlike other people, I have not forgotten who I am." And then suddenly the phone call has ended.

I stare at the phone, the same phone through which, moments ago, Mama sang to me.

I think back to that time so long ago, the time when Nadai died giving birth. Her mother threw all the grains and broke all the dishes. I remember the shard that I found, then stuck in my pocket. How good it felt to run this sharpness along my skin.

I wish I had this sharpness again, this relief.

Instead, all I have is my shame.

■ ■ ■

I CALL KEIJI SEVERAL more times over the following day. Once Keiji is at work, cleaning an Arab woman's house to earn some money, but the rest of the time she is there caring for Mama. Her voice is always emotionless.

"Keiji, can you ask Mama about my brothers and sister? Does she know their whereabouts?"

"Poni, your mama does not answer my questions anymore. She breathes still, but she is no longer bound to the earth."

"She can't speak?" I ask sadly.

"No," Keiji replies. "However, I can tell you this. When I first met up with your mother, and we decided to travel to Egypt together with a group of other villagers, she told me that she believed both of your brothers to be dead. Of course she thought you were dead, too. I do know for certain that your little sister died. She died while your mother walked."

I try to picture Mama putting Achii's little body down on the ground, laying her down like a bundle of sticks.

I ask Keiji to let me sing to Mama. "Please, just put the phone to Mama's ear once more." Keiji does this, and I sing every song I can think of, all the songs I used to know when I was a child.

The following day, Mama is dead. My heart is so heavy with grief that I can barely move. And yet I must. Somehow I must continue my journey.

—27—

SISTER HANNAH'S COMPOUND manager gives me a lift
to the Jomo Kenyatta airport, and I arrive six hours in advance of my flight. Sister has told me that I must be prepared for things that might go wrong at the last minute.

True to her imaginings, there is an Ethiopian passenger
in front of me sobbing to the person at the Kenya Airways
ticket counter.

"Please," she cries out. "I am scheduled to fly today.
Here is my letter of confirmation." She waves the letter as
if doing so will somehow remedy the situation. "Do you
need my identification card? I have it."

Meanwhile, her husband stands silently next to her, his
face trying its best to seem calm, to mask the weight of
disappointment.

The whole time they are talking, I am wondering if
my flight will also be canceled. Worse still, I am wondering whether there will be a problem with my paperwork.
Sometimes there are land mines where you least suspect
them. And maybe I wasn't really meant to leave the country. Maybe they will send me back.

When it comes my turn to step up to the counter, though,

the agent hands me my ticket. I put the ticket in my pocket but do not stop touching it, even for a moment. Even when I go to use the toilet, I am still touching the ticket with my fingers.

Then I am boarding an airplane. As the airplane starts to leave the ground, I feel as though I am being pulled away from my stomach. I want to scream out, but I do not. Instead I pray. Please, God, stay with me. I remember how hard it was to slow down enough to pray when I was a child. But now I do. Now I know how.

The airplane continues to rise into the sky. I think back to the night when I fled from my village. I was sure I was flying. And now here I am, once again rising.

As we enter into the sky, I look down at Africa stretched out below me like a big blanket made of green and brown patches. Pictures of my childhood flash before me — Nadai and me shaking the branches of the mango tree, herds of giraffes running, Mama grinding sorghum, my teacher peering at me through his oversized glasses, Kakuma with its endless queue of people waiting for food, Lokure under a blue scarf. And me running, always running.

And then, suddenly, these images disappear, and all I see are clouds.

As the airplane swims through the air, and as the hours pass, my eyes slowly close, and as I fall into sleep, I dream of Mama.

She is wearing a bright red dress and, catching my eye, she laughs. I reach for her, but she evades my grasp. She dances past me, her dress a swirl of red.

■ ■ ■

MORE GETTING IN AND OUT of airplanes, more pummeling through the sky until I have lost all sense of time and place.

Then, just as I think these plane rides will never end, we land in Denver. Dizzy, I get off the plane, my feet wobbly and unsure of themselves. I have no idea where to go.

I am supposed to meet a representative from the organization that has sponsored me, but the airport is huge and overwhelming with stores and people everywhere. Where should I find her?

I begin to blindly follow a crowd of people, all of whom seem to be moving in the same direction like migrating wildebeests. I continue to follow them as they board a train heading to the main terminal.

Next, there is a stairway that moves on its own. I am nervous at first, but I stand aside for a few moments and watch how people get onto it. I do as they do and hop on myself. Up I go, riding upwards, ascending into the unknown.

The first thing I see when I arrive at the top and step off is an enormous fountain, spewing water in all directions. However tough life is in America, and surely it will be, some of the rumors about this country must be true. Clearly water is so abundant here that it can be sprayed about and used for decoration. It is hard to believe.

All at once, I see a white woman holding a sign with my name on it. Indeed, she is from the African Center and, as she walks towards me, her dangly earrings swinging, she smiles and reaches out to shake my hand. Her pale hand is surprisingly firm. I cannot believe I have found her, that my coming here has actually worked.

"Good! You've arrived. My name's Susan. I'm so excited to meet you, Poni! I know you must be so tired and overwhelmed from your flight." The woman talks rapidly, as though she is happy and apologetic at the same time.

I look around. For some reason, I can no longer remember which direction I came from. All I see are people walking this way and that. It is as though the crowd has swallowed my path. I pick up my suitcase and begin to follow the woman.

"What a trip you've had," Susan says, turning towards me, and I nod. Such a long trip indeed. "I want to hear all about it," she assures me. She grabs my suitcase from me before I have a chance to protest. I am not used to having someone else carry my load. It is strange to suddenly feel this light.

I have never met this woman Susan before, and yet I get the feeling that, down the line, I will tell her everything, my whole story, even the not-so-pretty parts of it.

For the first time, I think I may want to.

I will not forget those I have left behind. If I could I would shout all the way back to Africa: "I have come first so that you may follow, my sisters." Yet I do not look behind me. Rather, I continue to follow Susan out of the airport and into my new country, to walk into sunshine so bright that I can barely see.

True, I am frightened, and yet, at this moment, I feel so very strong.

ON JULY 9, 2011, Southern Sudan achieved independence from Northern Sudan. Peace is still tenuous and
fragile, but the people of Southern Sudan are filled with
hope.

Authors' Note

Laura DeLuca and I first met at a conference in Denver in 2007. This conference brought together Southern Sudanese women from all over the world. These women were at the conference to share a message that females, not just males, were essential to the government and the future of Southern Sudan.

Laura was a presenter at the conference, while I was attending the conference to do research. Drawn in by the question of why so much attention had been given to the Lost Boys while the Lost Girls' stories had, for the most part, gone untold, I was trying to write a book about the women.

In fact, the women I met at the conference did have amazing stories. However, after hearing them, I realized there was a great deal I did not know or understand about the Sudanese culture. After speaking with Laura, I saw an opportunity for a wonderful partnership. I could do the writing, while Laura, who knows East Africa extremely well, who is an anthropologist, and who has worked with the Sudanese community for many years, could help me with the details of language, culture and history.

Together, Laura and I discussed what format would work best for sharing the women's stories. We decided that fiction would allow us to weave together the greatest number of experiences at once.

Though the women we spoke with were generous and open in sharing their stories, because many of them were very young when they had to flee their villages, and because many experienced a great deal of trauma, remembering was often a painful or difficult experience. Fiction allowed us to fill in gaps, string stories together and focus on themes. Poni is a created, composite character, but she is based on the resiliency and perseverance of all of the women we spoke with. These women possess a determination to survive, get an education and give back to their nation — a determination that inspired and continues to inspire us.

— Leah Bassoff

Who Are the Lost Children of Sudan?

The Lost Boys and Girls of Sudan are orphans who fled the violent attacks on Southern villages during the second Sudanese civil war, which started in 1983. Some of these children trekked thousands of miles before they reached Kakuma, a United Nations refugee camp in Kenya. Once there, they continued to suffer from starvation, dust storms and lack of health care.

The young boys were dubbed the Lost Boys by foreign-aid workers, who associated them with the parentless boys in *Peter Pan*.

The Lost Girls were less visible than the Lost Boys when US State Department representatives visited the Kakuma camp. Unlike the young men who lived together in a section of the camp for unaccompanied minors, the girls had been placed with ad hoc Sudanese foster families and so they were less conspicuous. These "families" were often hesitant to part with the girls, who represented the possibility of a large bride price consisting of cows and cash. Moreover, when the United Nations High Commissioner for Refugees (UNHCR) consulted Sudanese leaders at Kakuma to assist in decisions about which youths should be resettled, the male elders favored boys over girls. According to the elders, the Sudanese boys were better candidates for traveling abroad and would be more likely than girls to attend school in the US.

For these reasons, among others, in 1999, the State Department decided to allow nearly 4,000 Lost Boys to resettle in the US, but only 89 girls.

Eventually, Refugees International urged the US government and the UNHCR to work together to resettle more unaccompanied females. Some Lost Girls were selected for resettlement as early as 2001. These girls had the luck, as well as the burden, of being some of the few fortunate enough to escape an otherwise often dire fate.

Although Southern Sudan became independent in 2011, life is still very difficult for girls there, and a girl is still more likely to die in childbirth than to graduate from school.

Our hope, in writing this book, is that more girls will get to tell their stories, receive educations and take on leadership roles. Since the signing of the peace accord in 2005, more than two million refugees have returned to South Sudan. Others have chosen to remain, at least temporarily, in the United States in order to pursue their educations. Whether or not they will eventually return to Sudan, all of the young women we spoke with remain connected to their country. They know that they are the hope and future peace for the Republic of South Sudan.

ACKNOWLEDGMENTS

The Sudanese have a saying — "One hand cannot clap."
We received so much help and support from our community. Special thanks go to Jean Wood, Sharon and Rich Wildau, Gretchen Stein, Lindsay Eppich, Dana James, Marilyn Krysl, Tom Maddox, Ed Stackler, Richard Klin, Elisabeth Kerr, Eben Weiss, Jennifer Dickerson, Pam Holloway-Sheldon, Laurie Felland, Aaron Couts, Ian Morgan, Beth Novick, Marc Gale, Linda Block, Hannah Payne, Minja Maletic, Kathy Collins, Hope Forgey, Nii Armah Sowah, Joan Gabriele, May Penuela, Mara Goldman, Jim Schechter, Katherine Bruch, Alphonse Keasley, Priya Jha, Ajume Wingo, Eric Wirba, Myanna Lahsen, Shoba Rajgopal, Tracy Ferrell, Bridget Kromrey, Colleen Scanlan-Lyons and Jeff Lyons, Carol Conzelman, Alicia Davis, Lori Hunter, Nicole Smith, Jane Sovndal, Carmela Weber, Eliza Woloson, Francoise Mbahazi, Leyla Day, Diane Sieber, Rift Valley Institute (RVI), School for Advanced Research in Santa Fe, Paul Shankman, Mariella Bacigalupo, Priscilla Craven, Ursula Lauper, Deborah Fryer, Terry and Judith McCabe, Sharon Campbell, Weston Roberts, Jackie Holder, Elizabeth Scarborough, Peter Gwinn, Simone Charles, Judith Jackson, Jo Driessen, David Fleming, Tim Zych, Raphael Mungai, Stefano Ponte and Lisa Richey, Mr. Mbiji, the late Eugene Bodo, Pete O'Neal and Charlotte O'Neal, Maggie Duncan Simbeye, Gabriel Ole Saitoti and family, Maanda Ngoitiko, Jordan Olmstead, Jordan Campbell,

Susan Kelly, John Ryle, Corinne Kratz, Michael McGovern, Sylvester Maphosa, Julie Maximom, Lina Bahn, Kim Mattingly, Paige Eldridge, Cecile McAninch, Mary Rolinson, Katie Chiocchio, Tim Braughn, Dave Secunda, Jeff Lyons, the alumni of the Global Seminar Tanzania, Cloud Baffour, students from the Regional Cultures of Africa (ANTH 1150), Peter Simons, Beth Osnes, Susan Clarke and Gary Gaile, Rachel Silvey and Dylan Clark, Kamala Kempadoo, Laura Busse, Judy Huston, Elizabeth Dunn, Rabbi Bronstein, Katie and Mark Milleker, Jon Sheldon, Joy Ann Sofio, John Maluccio, John Engels, Rain Donahue, Liz Johnson and Curtis Altmann and the RPCV Kenya Teachers of 87-89, the Bynum family, the Pasquini family, the Nelson family, the DeLucas, the Madtsons, the Paynes, the Wirths, the Frasers, the Kovachs, Jose Del Pino, the Hobart-Frank family, the Heiderers, the Vargas, the Hernandez family, the Lazaroby family, the Alaimos, the Sandbower family, the Accordinos, the Medlers, the Bhatia family, the Bramer/Thompson family, Matthew Gumpert, the Brennig family, Elizabeth O'Malley, Susan Erikson, Brian and Erica King, Urban Hamid, Ursula Lauper and Christina Lee.

Our family members have given us endless emotional and editing support along the way: Evelyn and Bruce Bassoff, Linda and Michael DeLuca, Jennie and Ned Oldham, Bart and Sarah DeLuca, Kurt Scholler and Katherine Alaimo, Carol and Charlie Alaimo.

Thanks to our incredible and supportive husbands: Ethan Lovell and Chris Alaimo.

To our wonderful boys: Kevin and Avery Lovell and Charlie and Simon Alaimo. We love you boys more than words can say.

Thanks also go to the wonderful schools in which Laura and I are privileged to teach: The University of Colorado at Boulder and Denver Montclair International School.

To our amazing agent, Matthew Carnicelli, to whom we owe

everything. To our fabulous editors, Shelley Tanaka and Sheila Barry, who helped shape and nurture this book. Your sage and thoughtful editing was an absolute gift.

Most of all, thank you to the community of Southern Sudanese women and men who graciously shared their stories with us and who taught us about survival, hope and grace.

Brief Timeline of Sudan

1899-1955 Sudan is under joint British-Egyptian rule.

1955 There is a large secessionist movement in the South, called the Anyanya. The first civil war begins and lasts until 1972.

1972 Under the Addis Ababa peace agreement between the government and the Anyanya, the South becomes a self-governing region.

1978 Oil is discovered in Bentiu in Southern Sudan.

1983 Civil war breaks out again in the South, involving government forces and the Sudan People's Liberation Movement (SPLM) led by John Garang. The second civil war lasts until 2005. President Jaafar Nimeiri declares the introduction of Islamic sharia law.

1989 The Sudanese government begins deploying army militia to raid villages in the South.

1992 The Kakuma Refugee Camp in northwestern Kenya begins accepting Sudanese refugees. This camp has since expanded to serve refugees from Somalia, Ethiopia, Burundi, the Democratic Republic of Congo (DRC), Eritrea, Uganda and Rwanda.

1999 Almost 4,000 Sudanese refugee boys are approved for resettlement to the United States.

2002 Government and the Sudan People's Liberation Army

(SPLA) sign a ceasefire agreement providing for a six-month renewable ceasefire in the central Nuba Mountains, a key rebel stronghold.

2003 The Darfur conflict reignites.

2005 Government and Southern rebels sign a peace agreement that includes a permanent ceasefire. Former Southern rebel leader John Garang is sworn in as first vice president. A constitution is signed — one that gives a large degree of autonomy to the South. On July 30, John Garang is killed in a helicopter crash. He is succeeded by Salva Kiir Mayardit.

2009 Leaders of the North and South agree on the terms of a referendum on independence.

2011 Southern Sudan gains independence and becomes its own nation. The Republic of South Sudan is founded on July 9, 2011.

FOR MORE INFORMATION

Although little has been written about the Lost Girls, there are a number of books, films and plays about the Lost Boys:

A Great Wonder: Lost Children of Sudan. Bullfrog Films, 2004.
A documentary directed by Kim Shelton, about two Lost Boys and one Lost Girl who are adjusting to their new life in Seattle.

Applegate, Katherine. *Home of the Brave.* New York: Feiwel and Friends, 2007.
A novel in verse about Kek, a young Sudanese refugee who joins his aunt's family in Minnesota.

Benjamin and His Brother. 2002.
A documentary by British filmmaker Arthur Howes, about Benjamin and William Deng, brothers in a Kenyan refugee camp who are separated when only one is accepted by a US resettlement program.

Bixler, Mark. *The Lost Boys of Sudan: An American Story of the Refugee Experience.* Athens, GA: University of Georgia Press, 2005.
A nonfiction book by a journalist about Lost Boys who moved to Atlanta.

Bol, Aher Arop. *The Lost Boy: The True Story of a Young Boy's*

Flight from Sudan to South Africa. Roggebaai, South Africa: Kwela, 2009.
The autobiography of a Lost Boy who makes his way from Sudan through Ethiopia, Kenya, Tanzania, Zambia and Zimbabwe to South Africa.

"Breach," *NCIS: Los Angeles.* Season 1. 2011.
An episode that concerns a Sudanese refugee and his past links to the Sudan People's Liberation Army (SPLA).

Carter, Lonnie. *The Lost Boys of Sudan.* New York: Broadway Play Publishing, 2011.
A play that takes place in the Kakuma Refugee Camp and in a high school in Fargo, Minnesota. First performed by Children's Theater Company, Minneapolis, in 2007.

Childers, Sam. *Another Man's War: The True Story of One Man's Battle to Save Children in the Sudan.* Nashville: Thomas Nelson, 2009.
A book about Childers' work with Sudanese war orphans in Africa. His story was also turned into a film, *Machine Gun Preacher*, 2011, directed by Marc Forster.

Coates, Jan L. *A Hare in the Elephant's Trunk.* Markham, ON: Red Deer Press, 2010.
A novel based on the life of Jacob Deng, now living in Nova Scotia.

Dau, John Bul, and Michael Sweeney. *God Grew Tired of Us: A Memoir.* Washington, DC: National Geographic, 2007.
The story of John Dau, also chronicled in the 2006 documentary directed by Christopher Dillon Quinn and Tom Walker, about three Lost Boys who migrated to the United States.

Deng, Benson, Alephonsion Deng, Benjamin Ajak and Judy A.

Bernstein. *They Poured Fire on Us From the Sky: The True Story of Three Lost Boys of Sudan.* New York: PublicAffairs, 2005.
Told in their own words, the true story of the fourteen-year journey of three Lost Boys who came to the US in 2001 before 9/11.

Dinka Diaries. 2005.
A documentary by Filmon Mebrahtu about Lost Boys in Philadelphia.

Duk County: Peace Is in Sight in the New South Sudan. 2013.
A documentary about the efforts of now grown Lost Boy John Dau to provide a clinic, and the work of Dr. Geoff Tabin and Dr. Alan Crandall's work to restore eyesight to residents in the Dinka area of Duk County. Directed by Jordan Campbell.

Eggers, Dave. *What Is the What: The Autobiography of Valentino Achak Deng.* San Francisco: McSweeney's, 2006.
A novel based on the story of Valentino Achak Deng, now living in Atlanta. The novel documents the many struggles Achak faced both in the United States and in Sudan and Kenya.

Hecht, Joan. *The Journey of the Lost Boys: A Story of Courage, Faith, and the Sheer Determination to Survive by a Group of Young Boys Called "The Lost Boys of Sudan."* Jacksonville, FL: Allswell Press, 2005.
The book describes the epic journey taken by the Lost Boys, beginning in their rural villages of Southern Sudan and ending with their arrival as young men in the United States. The book is written by the boys' American mentor, "Mama Joan."

Lomong, Lopez, and Mark Tabb. *Running for My Life: One Lost Boy's Journey from the Killing Fields of Sudan to the Olympic Games.* Nashville: Thomas Nelson, 2012.
The autobiography of the US Olympian and former Lost Boy.

Lost Boys of Sudan. 2003.
A documentary film directed by Jon Shenk and Megan Mylan, about two Lost Boys, Santino Majok Chuor and Peter Kon Dut, who came to the US. The film follows the Sudanese boys on their journey to Kakuma Refugee Camp and from there to the United States.

McMahon, Felicia R. *Not Just Child's Play: Emerging Tradition and the Lost Boys of Sudan.* Jackson, MS: University Press of Mississippi, 2007.
An anthropological analysis of the music, dance and folklore of the Didinga community living around Syracuse, New York.

Nhial, Abraham, and DiAnn Mills. *Lost Boy No More: A True Story of Survival and Salvation.* Nashville: Broadman & Holman, 2004.
The autobiography of Abraham Nhial, who fled to Ethiopia from Sudan.

Park, Linda Sue. *A Long Walk to Water.* New York: Clarion, 2010.
This story follows the intersecting lives of a Lost Boy and a girl in Sudan.

Pipher, Mary. "African Stories," in *The Middle of Everywhere: Helping Refugees Enter the American Community.* Orlando, Florida: Harcourt, 2002.
Pipher describes the "transformation" of her quiet hometown — Lincoln, Nebraska — after it is chosen as a "preferred community" for refugees. Lincoln becomes "a richer curry of peoples" as newly arrived refugees, including Lost Boys, settle there.

Rebuilding Hope. 2009.
A documentary, directed by Jen Marlowe, that follows three

Lost Boys as they return to South Sudan after being resettled in the US.

War Child. 2008.
A documentary, directed by C. Karim Chrobog, about the life of hip-hop musician and former child soldier Emmanuel Jal.

Yang, Daniel Cheng. *Kakuma Turkana: Dueling Struggles: Africa's Forgotten Peoples*. Saint Paul, MN: Pangaea, 2002.
A photographic journal of Kakuma Refugee Camp and the indigenous Turkana peoples of northwest Kenya.

Glossary

Acacia A genus of shrubs and trees common in the arid regions of Africa. Also known as a thorn tree.

Askari A Kiswahili word for guard or policeman.

Baobab A tree found in Africa, Australia and the Arabian Peninsula. Also called a monkey tree or upside-down tree.

Bari An ethnic group from the Equatoria region of South Sudan.

Batis A small bird common in sub-Saharan Africa.

Bongo One of the largest African antelopes. They are chestnut colored with white stripes.

Bozibozi A Kiswahili word meaning stupid or useless.

Changaa A Swahili word for alcohol made from palm sugar and yeast.

Chevdo A spicy Indian mix of nuts and potato crisps.

Didinga An ethnic group living in South Sudan close to the Ugandan border, near the Didinga Hills.

Duka A Kiswahili word for a small shop that sells incidental items such as packets of spice, laundry detergent and matches.

Garang, John The leader of the Southern Sudan People's Liberation Army (SPLA).

Guinea worm A long threadlike worm that is a subcutaneous parasite of humans and other mammals. The worm causes ulcer-like lesions on the legs and feet and can destroy tissue and muscle if untreated.

209

Igbo An ethnic group of southeastern Nigeria.

Jacaranda A sub-tropical tree native to South America; it has been widely planted in Africa because of its beautiful lavender flowers.

Kali A Kiswahili word meaning harsh.

Kiberiti Kiswahili for matches.

Kikuyu A powerful ethnic group in Kenya. Jomo Kenyatta, the first African president of Kenya, was Kikuyu.

Kimbo An East African brand of pure white cooking fat.

Kiswahili A language that combines Bantu and Arabic words.

Kitu kidogo A Kiswahili saying that literally means "little thing." It has come to refer to bribe money.

Latuka An ethnic group in the Equatoria region of South Sudan. Also referred to as Lotuko or Lotuka.

Lokembe A musical instrument played with the thumbs.

Lucozade An energy drink sold in East Africa.

Maale (sometimes spelled Male) A greeting in the Nuer language that is the equivalent of "How are you?" or, "Is there peace?" The response, "Maale madit," means "How are you and is it a big peace?"

Maasai (sometimes spelled Masai or Masaai) A Nilotic ethnic group of semi-nomadic people located in Kenya and northern Tanzania. Historically, they raised cattle for a living but now participate in farming and have migrated to urban areas to work as guards or in the mining industry.

Malaya A Kiswahili word for prostitute.

Mancala An East African game played with pebbles or seeds on patterned boards consisting of a number of pits arranged in two or four rows. These pits may be carved into wooden boards or scooped into the sand.

Médecins Sans Frontières / MSF (Doctors without Borders) A French humanitarian nongovernmental organization that has won the Nobel Peace Prize and is best known for its projects in war-torn and developing countries facing endemic diseases.

Merti A locally brewed Sudanese beer.

Miraa A flowering plant native to the Horn of Africa. Its bitter plant stem can be used as a stimulant, similar to caffeine.

Murahaleen An Arabic word that refers to the Baggara Arab tribal militia. It literally means "on the move." During the Sudanese civil war it referred to traveling members of the Arab militia.

Mwizi A Kiswahili word meaning thief.

Nuer A Nilotic ethnic group of South Sudan and western Ethiopia.

Peptang A tomato sauce popular in Nairobi. Peptang is a product line that produces sauces, spices and juices.

Red Army Youth members of the Sudan People's Liberation Army (SPLA), recruited to fight as child soldiers.

Safi A Kiswahili word that literally means clean, but the colloquial meaning is "good."

Samosa A fried or baked pastry with a savory filling such as spiced potatoes, onions, peas or ground beef.

Shamba A Kiswahili word for farm or garden.

Sharia The Arabic word for Islamic law.

Shifta A term used in Eritrea, Ethiopia, Kenya and Somalia; it means rebel, outlaw or bandit.

Shuka A Maasai word for a decorative fabric made of handwoven cotton, usually in bright red and blue plaid.

Simba Mbili Literally means "two lions" in Kiswahili; a popular brand of curry powder used in East Africa.

SPLA (Sudan People's Liberation Army) The rebel army that fought against the Sudanese government for independence.

Sukamawiki A Kiswahili word that literally means "push the week." It refers to green vegetables like collard greens that are less expensive to purchase than meat and thus help save the week's budget.

Taposa An ethnic group in South Sudan that primarily inhabits the Kapoeta region of Eastern Equatoria.

Tukul A round hut with a cone-shaped roof.

Turkana A nomadic pastoralist group from northwestern Kenya, whose land was used to form the Kakuma Refugee Camp.

Ugali A stiff maize porridge (a bit like polenta or grits) that is a staple food in Kenya, Tanzania and other East African countries.

UNHCR (United Nations High Commissioner for Refugees) The agency mandated to lead and coordinate international action to protect refugees and resolve refugee problems worldwide.

ABOUT THE AUTHORS

LEAH BASSOFF is a writer and teacher and a former assistant editor at Penguin. She has written for *Denver Voice* and *The Coloradan*. LAURA DELUCA teaches anthropology at the University of Colorado in Boulder. She has done extensive fieldwork in East Africa and has written articles on her experiences with Sudanese refugees in *Anthropology News*, *Anthropology Matters* and *Journal of Refugee Studies*. Leah and Laura met at a conference about Sudanese affairs and were compelled to combine their talents and expertise to work together and give voice to this previously untold story.

Leah and Laura live in Colorado.

LOST GIRL FOUND

Lost Girl Found

LEAH BASSOFF

AND

LAURA DELUCA

Groundwood Books
House of Anansi Press
Toronto Berkeley

Groundwood Books / House of Anansi Press
110 Spadina Avenue, Suite 801, Toronto, Ontario M5V 2K4
or c/o Publishers Group West
1700 Fourth Street, Berkeley, CA 94710

We acknowledge for their financial support of our publishing program the Government of Canada through the Canada Book Fund (CBF).

Library and Archives Canada Cataloguing in Publication
Bassoff, Leah, author
Lost girl found / by Leah Bassoff and Laura DeLuca.
Issued in print and electronic formats.
ISBN 978-1-55498-416-9 (bound).—ISBN 978-1-55498-418-3 (html)
I. DeLuca, Laura, author II. Title.
PZ7.P295Lo 2014   j813'.6   C2013-905646-7
                         C2013-907144-X

Cover illustration by Enrique Moreiro
Maps by Scott MacNeill
Design by Michael Solomon

Groundwood Books is committed to protecting our natural environment. As part of our efforts, the interior of this book is printed on paper that contains 100% post-consumer recycled fibers, is acid-free and is processed chlorine-free.

Printed and bound in Canada

RECYCLED
Paper made from
recycled material
FSC
www.fsc.org   FSC® C103567